A COWBOY CHRISTMAS

AN AMERICAN TALE

Praise for *A Cowboy Christmas An American Tale*

"It's good and it moves! Tom Van Dyke tells a rousing tale of a young man learning how to cowboy and finding the girl of his dreams. I've written a good 40 western stories but learned a lot from Tom's book."

— ELMORE LEONARD
Novelist

"INSPIRING. *A Cowboy Christmas An American Tale* reveals the true American West but goes even further. A man and woman who refuse to let a soaring relationship disappear is a sign of life on earth at its best."

— MICHAEL BLAKE
Author of *Dances With Wolves*

"*A Cowboy Christmas* is a wonderful tale of a young cowboy's roam and a heartfelt love story. A great Christmas story and a delightful read for all seasons."

—THOMAS COBB
Author of *Crazy Heart*

"I'm a narrative painter, so as I read this book, the words drew pictures in my mind. These images are vivid and the story feels real. *A Cowboy Christmas An American Tale*, is a welcome addition to my library."

— HOWARD TERPNING
Western Artist

"A GREAT RIDE!"

— BOB BOZE BELL
True West magazine

"*A Cowboy Christmas* is a warm, well-written tale of a young man discovering himself and the new world during an engaging adventure in the American West. The book took me back in time and sparked memories of when I was working on Western films with my friend John Wayne."

— DON COLLIER
Western Film and TV Actor

"*A Cowboy Christmas An American Tale* is a beautiful story for all ages. Not since the work of James Dickey have I read such poetry in a novel. A wonderful remembrance for what the Old West once was. Don't wait for the film—buy the book now."

— KEN ROTCOP
Screenwriter-Producer

"Tom Van Dyke has crafted an inspired story of the Old West, Arizona and New Mexico Territories—1873. A well-researched tale of an adventuresome young man carving out a life that most men can only dream about. Hold on tight. It's a fast ride. This magical tale fits like a vintage Stetson and good pair of boots."

— MARSHALL TRIMBLE
Official Arizona State Historian

"I tasted the dust and lived the adventure of being on the Western frontier. The narrative arc, authenticity of the story, and fine-cut dialogue drew me in—captivating my imagination. I was there, enjoying every moment. Mr. Van Dyke is a most enjoyable wordsmith."

— CYNTHIA WEBER
School Teacher

A COWBOY CHRISTMAS

AN AMERICAN TALE

A Novel

TOM VAN DYKE

PAGE BRANCH PUBLISHING
PHOENIX, ARIZONA

Page Branch Publishing, Phoenix, Arizona

Fifth Edition 2015 revised and expanded with additions

A Cowboy Christmas An American Tale
is a work of historical fiction. Names, characters and events are products of the author's imagination. All characters, events, and any resemblance to persons, living or dead are coincidental.

ISBN 978-0-692-30112-8
ISBN 978-0-615-41555-0 (ebook)

Manufactured in the United States of America

1 3 5 7 9 10 8 6 4 2

Mary Van Dyke, Editor

Ellen Alsever, Story Editor

Douglas Carn, Text

Walker Van Dyke, Media & Design

Bob Coronato, Cover Art
"High Roller", Original Chine Colle' Etching

Please Support Our Libraries, Museums, and National Parks

Visit: ACowboyChristmas.com
for Special Features and Particulars

Audiobook and eBook available from these online providers:
Audible.com, Amazon.com, iTunes.com

For

Mary, who has inspired and shared every trail

And

Adam, Mark, Grant, Jocelyn, and Walker

who made it a joy

PREFACE

I have a long trail of praise for the American cowboy. Leafing through tattered pages of hand-written journals and dust-covered books, and wandering museums admiring masterworks of western artists, I looked beyond the golden frames as windows into America's past, and imagined what the restless spirit of the West was like one hundred fifty years ago for cowboys on the American frontier.

Inspired, I felt challenged to create a magical story that crisscrosses the expansion of the far West and collides with destiny—a story about cowboys who burned themselves like candles for experiences worth living and values that created strength and revealed character—a story as enduring as the romance of the West.

Embracing a cowboy's flavorful soup of words and expressions, WB tells his story with cowboy wit and humor. His tale begins in 1873. Not yet sixteen, with hope and dreams, he crosses the Mississippi, and without fear, leaves the far shore of civilization behind. With empty pockets, a spark for life, and a wild sense of freedom, he follows his heart searching for adventure and fortune and discovers the romance.

"Columbus discovered America in 1492
Horses arrived in 1519
Cattle arrived in 1521
Then there were C o w b o y s"

—tom van dyke

CONTENTS

A COWBOY CHRISTMAS

AN AMERICAN TALE

1

BLOWING IN THE WIND

"It is not in the stars to hold our destiny but in ourselves."
—WILLIAM SHAKESPEARE

BLOWING IN THE WIND, I wasn't much more than a hayseed, fifteen years old, when I stowed away on a wooden ship crossing the Atlantic Ocean from the old country. I was on the trail for adventure, discovery, and fortune in the new world. It was the year I gave up my gold and silver—1873. With the gold sovereign from my parents, I bought an Indian pony and a high-horned Mexican saddle from a trader. I traded the silver pocket watch my father had given me for an American rifle and I was off. I was looking to ripen in the far West.

Chasing the rainbow, I started my roam. I crossed the Mississippi and left the muddy bank of civilization as I knew it. Rumors of free land with vast riches, and the discovery of California gold lying on the ground no deeper than a carrot, had set off a stampede of white-hooded wagons migrating in pandemonium for the land of the setting sun.

The further I plowed from civilization the more of it I found. Furniture and other items of good intention too heavy for mule or ox to haul another day were left, picked over, and strewn along the trails. And then with certain predictability, miles up ahead, I'd find graves marked with headboards, and the bleached bones of an ox or horse that travelers were forced to slaughter for lack of food and planning. This was common sight.

Trail-weary mules would haul to a stand-off, refusing to budge. Negotiations began with a crack of the whip, followed by a barrage of verbal encouragements, blistering the ears of the mules and not fit for the lessons of Sunday school.

Another household item would sail from the prairie schooner.

Having rested for two hours and satisfied their terms had been addressed, the victors, with another crack of a whip, would launch a momentary charge up the trail. The dust would flood over the top of the wagon wheels and through the spaces between the loops of the canvas ties into the wagon.

This combined folly of tongue, temper, whip, and grunt created a sight that made the covered wagons appear to float like boats on billowing waves in clouds of dust.

Between the torrid sun and the relentless dust, faces burned and noses bled from the dry, cutting dust which covered every man, woman, and child —inside and out.

Not everyone's wagon made it across the vast prairie. At a point of no turning back, I passed a family downloading a heavy rosewood sideboard from their wagon to lighten the load. I stopped to help them. Admiring the beautiful family heirloom, mother ran her hand over the dusty top revealing the craftsmanship and fine, polished finish. She smiled with a distant gaze releasing memories and a time past. With a deep breath and as if she had suddenly remembered a forgotten chore, she turned quickly and returned to the wagon.

I watched as she stretched her boot to climb the wooden spokes. Pulling herself up hand-over-hand, she pushed off the hub to the top of the wheel and crossed over to take her place on the wooden seat of the wagon. Gripping the reins, her hands were cracked and calloused. Her beauty once bright and obvious, now of fewer years than thirty was fading with hardship and toil. Her lips were blistered and her fair skin parched, scrubbed by the wind, sun, and alkaline water.

Her striking eyes, the color of the ocean, were hardened with resolve in a steely gaze that left me with no doubt that with all the six-gun bravado and strength of the sombreros, the settlement of this hostile frontier would be carved out by the steadfast determination and courage of sunbonnets.

Having endured the endless solitude, monotony, and arid expanse of the Great Plains, I slowly approached the foothills of the Rocky Mountains.

Overcome by thirst, I was losing my song and enthusiasm for the lore of the West.

The trail was cluttered with believers and sorry settlers, Yankee neighbors, Rebel brothers, white marauders, men with all the earmarks of bad company—and *me*.

Rising up in the foothills before me, stood a majestic woodland forest of pine spears guarding the blue horizon of paradise. Mountain streams swarming with trout cut through the dense thicket of ponderosa pines. Thundering waterfalls glistened, cascading down the rock face.

I was looking for a trail of worn passage I could follow westward. The startling hoop-and-holler, which I first thought were Indians, set me on a gallop of escape and safety.

I threw a quick glance back over my shoulder. They were three bandits, looking for loot—my horse, saddle, rifle, anything in my pockets worth a cent. With rebel yells and caps popping, they were gaining on me. Their bullets buzzed by my ears like flies.

If the likes of me was worth their charge, they had to be desperate.

The sound of their yells and the whiz bangs of their bullets startled my pony. And with the speed of an arrow, he wheeled sharply, almost running out from under me—a talent he had kept hidden from me till then. We blazed for cover in the tall pines.

The marauders were closing and their rounds splintered and shattered the bark of the dense maze of trees we were fast approaching. There was no room to fit or enter.

The stream with its roaring rapids was just ahead. If we tried to cross, we'd be sitting ducks. At the stream's edge, a narrow path used by elk, deer, and the Indian for passage over the mountain twisted up and followed the bank of the river. We slipped into the fortress of shaded cover. The low hanging pine bows whipped past us, stinging both our hides.

Our climb slowed to a fast walk, weaving about the switchbacks up the slope, drifting through patches of light streaming through the high branches of the cathedral pines. Rushing up behind us, I could hear the blundering bandits' grumbling the worth and effort of their campaign.

A rifle cracked lead—a branch snapped down smacking me loose from the saddle. My startled pony slipped, dislodging rocks and black soil that fell splashing into the river. As he stumbled to catch his footing, I desperately clung on looking over the sheer edge of the high-cut bank at the fierce deafening rapids of the river below.

The dense trail unraveled. Up ahead was a small clearing that glowed green. Surprised, my pony jerked with a sudden stop, wide-eyed and snorting. Two bear cubs scampered across the trail—they were not alone! The ROAR startled every living thing and shook birds from their roosts. Mother was ANGRY! We had just entered her home—uninvited.

I was trapped!

The awesome force of Nature lay in my path and the blazing gunfire and crime of bandits squeezed me from the rear.

Rising up to her full height of seven feet, with a reach to ten, she made a massive impression with snarling teeth. She was going to defend her cubs. With glaring yellow eyes, the silver-tipped hairs on her neck and humpback shoulders were up.

Moaning, swinging her head, the extended claws of her paws were ready to thrash.

Nervous and snorting, my pony pitched and danced around. I turned hearing the voices of the bandits rustling up the trail from below. I saw the flash of a rifle. The shot echoed, booming and bouncing off the surrounding cliffs and high peaks.

Momma moaned and glanced around to see the whereabouts of her two baby cubs.

The trap was sprung—the moment was now!

My pony reared up to challenge her size and bolted straight at the grizzly. I lunged forward with all I was worth and let out the 'rebel yell' I had just become acquainted with.

The grizzly was struck by the surprise of our charge and momentarily faltered as we pushed past her. With snapping teeth and a whirling swat, she busted me from the saddle.

I dangled over the edge of the high-cut bank of the river grasping onto the saddle horn. My throbbing bloody arm was still attached. Righting myself, we bolted up the trail with momma bounding on our heels.

With leaping strides, the nine hundred pound grizzly raced, covering ground—thirty yards, twenty, ten—closing faster than my heart beat. In five she'd be pulling us down. With my pony's last burst of strength, we dashed up and over the high-cut bank and vaulted thirty feet down into the deep waters of the river below.

The echoing roar of the grizzly standing on the high bank of the river's edge greeted us as we surfaced the water. My Indian pony was already swimming to the far edge. Red rivulets of blood streamed from the claw marks of my wound. The cold, clear water relieved the pain.

The grizzly swaggered along the steep bank, looking up and down for access. Rising up to her full magnificent height, she let out a shrilling ROAR!

My trail-wise pony made his way up the other side of the steep-winding slope of a pristine mountain wilderness, yet undefiled by the presence of man.

The scent of pine and wildflowers filled my head. As we climbed higher, the air thinned and became cooler. Above the high shadows of late afternoon, the tips of the tall pines glistened in the warm rays of the sun.

I approached the crest of the mountain at twilight. I sat there spellbound—gazing at the luminous light glazing the distant western landscape as if it were the *dawn of creation* itself.

The wild and free beauty before me rekindled my enthusiasm and spirit. Raw, heavy vapors rose in harmony from the valley floor up into the glowing atmosphere of boiling red clouds. I watched the shimmering afterglow mesmerized as the theater of light slowly faded into a starlight encore that twinkled and glowed with brilliant constellations and blazing shooting stars.

2

A THIN LINE

THE NEXT MORNING I awoke to a new dawn rising. Glorious! . . . A new day in a new world.

I discovered a mountain man's log cabin pitched high on the western slope with inspiring views of lakes, canyons, and pine-clad cliffs.

The shelter was primitive and crudely built of logs by a trapper who must have had a hide as thick as bark to withstand the blowing winds and heavy snows of the freezing mountain-top winters.

Inside was low down and close quarters, just big enough for a three-legged aspen chair, a tree stump table, and a bed made with posted rails strung with rawhide rope and covered with hides. There was a grease light—a dish of tallow with a rag in it used as a candle.

Dusty yet orderly, it contained basic food stores for his return: cornmeal, flour, salt and pepper. A cast-iron skillet rested on the stump. I lifted the cover and found a round tin. I opened the tin and inside was a spool of line and a fish hook.

Fanning their fins in the clear, cool water, the native trout would dart out of sight under cover of the banks at the first sight of an intruder. I had learned at an early age to fish the brooks and lakes with my father and grandfather. Avid anglers, I think my grandfather could talk to the fish—he certainly thought like them: "Laddie, your every motion should mirror nature in approaching their world.

"They are wise, skittish creatures. Your close attention to the smallest detail is required. The soft and boggy banks shivers the water with vibrations from harsh, clumsy movements and pounding footsteps warning the fish of your presence."

Out of sight, back off from the banks, I carefully placed the worm on the sharp hook so the ends would wiggle lively in front of the trout's nose.

With a wiggle on the hook and the line tied to a long, thin aspen whip, I crouched down low and with light steps slowly approached the bank of the stream—careful not to disturb the brush. I took a silent position hidden behind the cover of a bush at the water's edge.

I watched the fast water hugging the bank on the far side of the stream. Reaching over the bank with my long fishing pole, I cast the line upstream and let the worm float naturally with the force of the current over the cold gravel bottom. The thin line glistened and stretched out. The worm whirled down the riffle sinking into the underwater pool where trout are most likely to be found.

As it swirled around the eddy, the tip of the aspen pole twitched. The line went taut with a series of sharp tugs. The whip bowed. I lowered the tip so the trout would not feel the pull of the pole on the line and become aware of my play. Then, I lifted the tip again, slowly drawing the slack out of the line and when I felt the fish solid—I struck quick with a jerk setting the hook and connecting me with the trout.

The trout surged with a full pull of the hook rising, splashing—bursting the surface of the water. The spring and action of the aspen whip I had selected made for an engaging contest. A battle of twists and flips, I worked and played to tire and land the trout without breaking the line. . . .

With an upward swing of my whip, a good breakfast sailed through the air landing on the green moss of the bank.

I enjoyed the sport of life's thrilling challenge connected by a thin line.

I acquired a liking for the high life and the taste of fresh mountain trout as I nursed my arm and regained my strength. My wounds were nearly healed. I wore the scar of the four claw marks as a badge of courage.

On the lakeshore, my breakfast trout filled the skillet and sizzled over the hot coals of a small fire when I noticed the flash of approaching lightning. A summer thunderstorm with gusty winds rolled in howling across the mountain's canopy of high pine.

In a wild rush, I climbed to the very top of a swaying, bending pine in order to experience the full fury of the storm. Whistling and wailing, with crashing torrents of freezing rain, I was whipped and shaken and flipped about by the thrilling hand of Nature. I enjoyed the sport of blowing in the wind. I felt mighty. I felt strong and that my life was unfolding before my eyes raising the question —was life streaming into me or out of me.

On the rough face of that mountain, I *had* come alive.

Tossing and twisting in my sleep, I woke to a full moon and decided to leave the mountain fortress that very night fearing I may not want to leave the pure air and inspired way of this virgin retreat in the light of day.

I saddled up my Indian pony, "You're the reason I'm still alive, partner. You saved my life . . . apparently you know where you're going." I climbed aboard, "Arrow, take me there."

We wandered slowly down out of the moonlit shadows of the towering pines—

3

INTO A MIRAGE

—INTO A MIRAGE of blazing hot light, a vast Sonoran landscape of thorny plants with showy flowers and giant saguaro cactus lay before me.

There was no water. There was no shade. . . .

Beads of sweat rolled off my forehead. I gazed across a harsh flatland populated with proud colorful lizards wearing scaly armor, sunning themselves on the hot rocks and asked myself: How could anyone—anything—survive out there? . . .

With a prayer asking for our safe passage, we started. "Come on partner . . . Arrow, let's go." He didn't move. I kicked him with my heels, "Git-up!" Nothing . . . "Arrow!" He shook his head, backed, turned, and wandered over into the shade of a scrub mesquite tree and planted himself. . . .

"Good idea, we'll wait for the sun to set."

We traveled at night by the light of the moon when the desert cooled and bloomed with eerie beauty. The desert came alive with life: bobcats, jack rabbits, rodents, snakes, lizards, and beetles—ready to eat . . . or be eaten. Owls hunted with silent wings. Coyotes howled—two sounded like seven. They ate anything they could chew.

Arrow had a slow steady pace and a nose always in search of water. We hadn't seen a trail or person for days—weeks.

The moon rose full, illuminating the desert as if it were the light of day. As I rode along, something most unusual appeared—something I never saw before and never again. I wondered if it was my imagination. I watched as an orange-red light slowly washed over the face of the moon until the moon was totally covered in a beautiful red glow. It was an amazing sight to behold. . . .

As the rising sun burned off the blue shadows of morning, I became aware of a faint, far-off squeaking sound. Miles ahead, I approached three covered wagons traveling west with a squeaky wheel.

For safety and good company, I thought it best to attach myself to the wagon train. I was loping by when I noticed her brushing her hair in the back of the wagon. *Oh my!*—she was made of sugar.

I slowed Arrow to a walk and her wagon passed me by. Keeping up alongside with the rolling wagon, I removed my hat and said, "Hello. Allow me to introduce myself."

"Hello," she smiled.

In a breath she stole my heart.

I loved her at first sight. Ginny had long flowing golden hair, divine eyes, sculpted features, and cherry lips.

We talked and laughed. Smart and witty, she was raised on books and in time we discovered each other. . . .

We worked for our supper. I gathered up wood for our cook fires and Arrow found water.

Over time the squeaking became annoying. Ginny's father appeared instantly, the moment I rigged a rawhide pouch that dripped a thick mixture of soap and bacon grease onto the hub, silencing the squeaking wheel grinding on the axle of their wagon. And with a nod Virgil said, "Pretty clever, boy."

Stargazing and cuddling by campfires with Ginny, we studied the heavens and watched the shooting stars leave trails in the sky. "There's the Big Dipper," pointed Ginny.

"Right beside Polaris, the North Star," I said.

"And together they are the timekeepers for the heavens," said Ginny. "The Big Dipper rotates counter-clockwise around the North Star every twenty-four hours." Holding her hand above her head, she clinched her fist, pointing her forefinger straight up as the handle of the Dipper. "It's ten o'clock now and the Dipper is here." Moving her hand, "At midnight it will be here; at two a.m. it will be here."

Reaching over, I cupped my hands into a bucket of water. "This is for you, Ginny." I held my hands out to her.

"What's for me?"

"Look." Ginny leaned in and peered at the moon's reflection in the water cupped in my hands.

"Oh! . . . Is this a promise?"

Gazing at Ginny in the glow of the full moon, she looked like a porcelain doll.

"Promise?" I asked. It was the first time a girl had ever gazed upon me with such loveliness, opening feelings of passion to me and my emotions.

"Are you promising me the Moon?"

I delighted in her gaze. Our back-and-forth volley in that tender moment was my awakening. Her glow gave my heart flight. So pure she was, I fumbled for words rising to her poetry. . . .

"I promise you the Moon, and under all the stars in heaven, I will love only you all the days of my life."

Her smile captured me and we held each other close for a long time when Ginny whispered, "My heart belongs to you."

We were inseparable. And, in the tall grass, we stole away. It was the happiest time of my life.

And Ginny wasn't far behind. She told her mother, "He loves me Mama and I love him."

"No you don't, Ginny! How do you know?" Concerned, "How can you tell?"

"His eyes tell me. The way they lay on me. He's strong and smart too." Ginny was passionate, "I have feelings for him Mama, his lips, his—"

"Hush child, you froth too much," putting her hands to her ears.

Ginny had a natural innocence that required vigilance and for her folks to be on constant watch for coyotes.

Her father took one look at WB and knew: tall, lean, and good-looking, he's on the loose.

We were rumbling around in the back of the covered wagon out of view. Ginny's mama was driving the team. Ginny was giggling and laughing when Mama yelled back, "Virginia, what's goin' on back there?"

". . . Nothin', Mama."

Well, Mama let out a whistle that could cut glass. "Virgil," she squalled, "Ginny's bundling up again."

We scampered, getting ourselves together knowing the chaperone was on his way, a big man with an Arkansas toothpick.

Lickety-split, I climbed out of the work end of the covered wagon, untied my pony that was trailing along and jumped on. By the time Pa busts up, I was a choirboy with my harmonica, serenading my prairie rose.

He flashed around the big knife, gesturing he's going to shave me real close.

"Oh, Pa, W's just playing me a melody."

If looks could kill, I had just been wounded.

Squinting hard and drawing the toothpick under his eyes, "Walker Brady, I'm eyein' you, boy." Slowly, Pa put the big knife back into its sheath and rode back up ahead. Ginny smiled and I trotted along with my serenade.

"I don't think your pa likes my music."

4

DANCING WITH PAIN

THE ARIZONA TERRITORY was opening up and we were on an ancient Indian trail used by the Apache and the Yavapai. The military out of Fort McDowell had widened the trail into a wagon road as a short cut to the West and the goldfields of California.

Word coming back down the trail from weary travelers returning to the United States, was that we were a day out from where the trail splits off.

Mrs. Hart and Virgil shared their food goods with one desperate family short on supplies. In return they gave us precious water they had drawn from the bubbling springs of Cave Creek.

I dipped a ladle of the water from their wagon's water barrel and shared it with Ginny—it had the most refreshing and unforgettable taste.

A young military man, riding on horseback, approached our moving wagons. Virgil was the wagon master riding lead. Virgil saluted him. "Good morning, soldier."

The soldier returned Virgil's salute. "Good day, sir. Snappy salute, you military?"

"Sergeant Major, retired. Thank you, soldier. You're coming from where we're going. Is it safe?"

"No, sir! With three wagons, I'd turn around. Attach yourself to a bigger train—safety's in numbers."

"We're looking for where the trail divides off towards Phoenix, Wickenburg, the gold fields—"

"And Indians. Straight ahead," added the soldier. "Their attacks are random and often—they'll find ya. The trail you're lookin' for splits off just beyond Black Mountain and is marked by a giant hellcat cactus."

"That's the one we're lookin' for."

"It'll bite ya. We went around it when we widened the road. A sharp fortress of thorny, hitch-hiking fruits with sharp barbs that pierce clothing, and draw blood with penetrating pain to arms and legs—a miserable bloody pain it is."

"We'll watch out for it."

"Don't let it kiss ya," laughed the soldier. "Travelers are always leaving personal items and notes on it for members of their party bringing up the rear."

"That's us, bringing up the rear. We're looking for a note telling us which trail our wagon train chose and we'll be catching up."

"Better hurry then, sir! Apaches are about."

It was late afternoon. I was poking along on my pony. The girl of my dreams, pretty as a picture in sundress and bonnet, was framed in the canvas at the rear of the covered wagon. She could hardly keep her eyes off me. Our passions were again suddenly interrupted when I noticed four Indians with rifles taking position undercover up on a knoll. They'd been dogging our lumbering wagons all morning and now they were setting up ahead to swoop down and ambush.

"Apache! Get down," I warned Ginny. I quick-kicked Arrow to a gallop and rode up alongside the wagons to warn the others. "—Apache! —Apache! —Apache!"

Up ahead on the dusty trail, the racing wagons were rolling around a sharp turn and the giant cactus tree that guarded the trail. I pulled up along-side the lead wagon just about the time it was passing the thorny, spiked sentry of the trail. The wagon jolted out of the wheel ruts, scaring my pony and I was thrown into the embrace of the messenger of pain. Captured and held in the nest of thorns, I hung there in agony and slowly untangled, falling and tumbling to the ground.

Now whether it was the commotion of seeing and fearing the Indians, or just Ginny's pa's way of saying goodbye, the dusty wagons kept rolling. I fell to the ground, covered with the thorny painful fruits from hell.

Rolling around, jerking and spinning in terrible anguish, I looked up and saw the Indians. Distracted from their ambush, they were no longer aiming their rifles at the wagons. They were laughing at me.

Covered with the thorny fruits, I tried to remove the barbs from my flesh, but the more I struggled, the worse it got. The barbed fruit stuck in my fingers, arms and legs, through my clothes, and appeared to be growing from my hat while my boots sprouted toes.

All the while, the laughing Indians watched my flailing painful dance. Lowering their rifles, they must have felt my agony . . . they mounted their ponies and rode off.

Lying there, the last thing I remembered was looking up and thinking that the cactus tree actually looked pretty with its golden thorns backlit by the setting sun.

Oh Lordy, it was not a silent night! I passed out into a nightmare of pain and soon encountered the devil's own flock—hairy-whiskered critters with a terrible stench. They sniffed, snorted, and dribbled, feasting on the buffet of cactus fruits. I was their banquet table. All night they roamed until they started nibbling at my toes.

Startled, I woke up. The black musk hogs of my dreams were eating the thorny fruits from my boots. They had plucked and eaten near every one from my body. As I rose up, they snorted and scampered off—praise the Lord.

Arrow had raced off with the wagons but, stayed faithful and returned. He grazed nearby. I got up slowly dusting myself off looking for thorns. Resting there in the cuff of my trousers, I spied a pearl button on a thread.

I looked over the giant cactus for a note. There was none. Carefully, I removed the few barbed fruits from my saddle blanket and crawled onto my pony.

I found the trail marker, a rickety wooden post slapped up with painted arrows, pointing the way to: Phoenix . . . Wickenburg . . . Gold Fields . . . and Indians. Looking over the crossroad, I tried to read which trail the wagons traveled and carried my true love away. With visions of fortunes to be made, the trails to both the gold fields and Wickenburg were well-tracked, leaving no clue to which route Ginny's wagon had traveled.

Slowly regaining full possession of my mind, I placed full blame for my misfortune squarely where it belonged, "Bonehead!" Arrow's ears perked straight up and he began to dance around. "Arrow, what were you thinking? Did you see what happened to me back there? Ginny's gone! . . . Which way did they go?"

Arrow settled and wisely looked over the trails from right to left. Giving him his head, he chose the trail to the gold fields.

Boy, was he wrong.

—

5

DUST TO DUST

MY TRUE LOVE had vanished. I found myself alone. Down and out, I took grunt work in the gold fields looking for pay dirt alongside the Chinamen. The grip of gold fever had every poor man believing that every shovel, every pan, and every blast would be the next mother lode, only to be left with empty pockets, shattered dreams, and a broken heart.

Washing gold from placer gravel was hard, unproductive work. Cleaning the blade of my shovel on the bank of the creek, I warmed myself by the supper fire, pondering a raw potato that I was lucky enough to stumble across. Bake it? Boil it? I didn't have a pot. Fry it? It was all up to me.

Sitting there—I got an uneasy feeling that something or someone was watching me. Looking around, I glanced across the stream. Rising slowly, I reached for my rifle. I could see shiny eyes in the shaded darkness of a coyote hole.

Caught staring, knowing he had been spotted, the old prospector elbowed his way out of his sleeping hole, not once taking his eyes off me or my potato. A raggedy man—gaunt, bent with hungry eyes fixed on my potato, splashed across the rivulet spoutin' gibberish and sat down in my company.

Eyeing the spud, he edged up closer and closer. He got so close I was catching his fleas and wearing his cologne. He was in an odd way. Before he sat in my lap, I put the potato down on a rock, halved it with my shovel and handed him half my supper.

Smiling he said, "Looky here." He took a spoon out of his overalls and feebly scooped out a large curl from his half of the potato. Reaching out, he asked me for the shovel. And then from the cuff of his pants he took a pinch of dusty gravel and sprinkled it onto the shovel, mixing it with what he explained later was mercury. He covered the sticky mixture in the hollow of his potato. Swinging the shovel my way, "Put yours on board," and I did.

While holding the shovel on the hot coals cooking our supper, he did his explaining, "Fire melts the amalgam and turns the mercury to vapor, which is leached off up into the baking potato leaving behind the gold."

The curl looked done and so did supper. Resting the shovel on a rock, the potatoes cooled down. Flipping over his potato with glee, "Magic!" Sure enough there was a button of gold. He flashed a big toothless smile, "Two for one, gold and supper." Admiring his magic he said, "Pick it up, feel the weight."

Stuck to the shovel, I freed it up with a stick

and picked up the warm metal. Flipping it around in my hand, it did have some heft. "Good trick," I said, handing the gold back to him.

"Keep it. Thank you for supper." We talked around for a while until he began to nod off. Watching him, I saw he had the bright eyes of a young man, yet he was old and weathered with heavy thoughts . . . He was asleep.

A night owl hooted and he was awake. "Gettin' late," he yawned, "I'm done in. Appreciate your company. I'll be packin' out in the mornin'." Rising slowly, he left me with, "You may want to think about leavin' too. This place just sands you down and fades your soul . . . 'Night."

"'Night, Birdy." I watched him leave. He turned, mustered a smile and walked, splashing away.

The next morning, I found him across the stream, slumped up against a tree. His cold blue eyes glistened—he was gone.

Placing the last of the big rocks to cover the old prospector in his sleeping hole, I used my shovel and filled in with gravel. Satisfied it looked natural and he would rest in peace, I climbed aboard Arrow and grabbed up my shovel. Turning to go, I took one last look over the creek and down at the rocks, "Rest your soul, sir," and I wandered off.

GINNY EASED QUIETLY from her bed covers so as not to wake her mother and father sleeping under their wagon. Their three wagons had circled up for the night with only one man on watch, warming himself by the glowing coals.

Unnoticed, she slipped out of her prairie dress

and stuffed it into a cloth sack and pulled out a book. Ginny was already dressed in trousers and boy's shirt. Looking down at her sleeping parents, Ginny took an envelope out of the book and put it on the seat of the wagon and weighted it with a stone.

She had carefully planned for this getaway. One of the mules stood off alone, bridled and ready for the taking. Quietly, she untied the rope hobble and led him off into the darkness of the night.

When they were a far distance away, she slung the sack around her neck and climbed on the bare back of the mule.

Her trek back to find WB had begun.

In the morning, Virgil frantically snapped the envelope off the seat of the wagon and opened it with a flick of his knife. Mrs. Hart leaned in close, took the letter from his hand and started to read:

"To my Father and adoring Mother,

I'm sorry to have to part from you in this way and I hope you forgive me for taking Roscoe. I know you would not release me if I asked, and I love you both. I will return one day soon with WB. Lily teams better with Buster anyway. If anyone can get a mule and ox to pull together, it is Father.

Your Loving Daughter,
Virginia"

Virgil, always the stoic one, and Mrs. Hart were sadly overwhelmed. In silence, with glazed, wet eyes, the reality of Ginny's letter sank in and Virgil said: *"Oh . . . my Ginny."*

6

SPARKS AND FUSES

MINING TOWNS sprang up overnight and just as fast turned to dust before building a church or a jail.

I roamed the gold fields, working and searching for the Harts. Panned out, I decided to head for the mines in the hills. Maybe they'd be there.

My job was to haul the ore carts in and out of the mine and empty the honey wagon.

For a ten-hour shift, each man was given four stubby candles to light his work in the drifts and tunnels of the mine. The candles didn't last for ten hours. So at meal break, twenty-five men blew out their candles and we ate, coughing in the infinite blackness of our tomb—to save wax.

Having just switched out an ore cart, I was lowered by lift into the throat of the mine. Creaking deeper and deeper into the pitch-black hole, I lit my candle and placed it on the honey wagon. Striking the floor of the shaft and about to enter the tunnel, I heard what I thought was the sound of swarming bees. Impossible, I thought.

I slowly rolled the honey wagon down the track past the glow of candles lighting up the dusty, sweaty faces of the miners and their work. Swinging ten-pound sledgehammers, punching holes and drilling tunnels through miles of rock, inch-by-inch, to collect gold hived in the veins of the earth was back-breaking work. So why were they smiling at me?

I began to feel like the canary in a sandbox of cats.

The hum filled the black tunnel as I rolled by the miners. Aiden, an Irish boy with red hair and my friend, stepped from the darkness into the candlelight. His violin was the source of the swarm. He smiled, bowing one long humming note, and winked. He could play the fiddle better than the devil himself.

He whipped into a hearty melody that inspired and lifted our spirits. The hammer men picked up on the beat banging on the rock walls, cart rails and timbers of the mine.

The music of the fiddle filled the mine and rolled over on itself echoing through the tunnels and the shafts.

The miners were ready for play. If they didn't have a hammer, they stomped their boots, clapped their hands or played their spoons. I could hear the swishing, side-by-side rhythm of pebbles on a metal sieve as I rolled by.

I pushed the honey wagon down the track. One of the miners jumped on the rolling wagon, swinging his hammer from side to side pounding on it like a big steel drum, Boom -- Boom - Boom. The low booming beats vibrated off the tunnel walls in concert with the fiddle. It was unbelievably beautiful.

"Walker," a voice called out.

Boom -- Boom - Boom.

"I'm coming."

"Walker."

Boom -- Boom - Boom.

My name was the verse, called out and thrown from miner to miner from one end of the mine to the other.

"Walker."

Boom -- Boom - Boom.

Their faces glowed and their performance overwhelmed me. Pushing the honey wagon to a stop, I noticed the burning fuses. The sparks from the hissing fuses raced to the explosive charges stuffed in the blasting holes of the tunnel. The men quickly backed off covering their heads with shovels. The fiddle played the funeral dirge. The miners watched, enjoying my panic . . . And, just when I was about to run, Bear Creek Joe, the powder man, snatched the fuses out of the blasting holes in the wall and handed them over to me.

I'd been played. They were all laughing. Aiden stepped forward and with a final flourish of the fiddle, and altogether with whistles, cheers, and clapping, the miners shouted, "Happy Birthday!"

Quite taken by their opera, I stood there speechless, holding the burning fuses sparking in my hand. Overcome with emotion I managed to say, "Thank you."

"Let's eat!" they shouted. And then they all returned to their stations and blew out their candles.

I was sixteen. . . .

GINNY WAS FIFTEEN—and lost. . . .

The first rays of sunrise had crest the mountain. Roscoe trudged slowly up the winding road to the mines with his head hung low. Ginny was slumped forward onto his mane with her arms around his neck. She slipped in and out of consciousness. Each plodding step was slower than the last until Roscoe stopped . . . he too was asleep.

"Hoppin' rabbits and elephant smoke! Looky, looky," said the big Negro woman cook. "My eyes are laughin' and my heart's breakin'. Child, ain't you a ragamuffin. Comes over here. Let Maddy get to ya fast 'fore them low fellows gets to dancin' 'round you!"

Maddy was a wonderful spirit of fifty years and once her mouth was engaged, she did not try to stop it. Wouldn't if she could. "Yes, you, on 'dat run-down, sorrowful mule. Master? Mistress? Pretty child, comes over here an' have a slice of Maddy's mince pie for ya falls off and finds you ain't dreamin'."

Ginny had her hair tucked up under a dusty bowler hat. She rose up exhausted, tipping and tired beyond sleep. She was awakened by the holler of a black woman standing over two skillets baking over firewood and waving a pie flipper motioning for her to come over and have a piece of pie.

Ginny dropped from Roscoe's back like a sack of rocks.

Maddy moved quickly and scooped up Ginny as easily as lifting a sack of meal. "Maybe we best start off with some rest, child." Hefting her in her arms, she carried Ginny to a tent behind her shack,

"Well you ain't no Johnny." She laid Ginny down on a cot, and her hat fell off. "More like a southern belle, I imagine." Ginny was asleep.

"Wake up girl! It's mornin'." Maddy poked her head inside the tent. "Nothin' gets done till you gets to doin'." Ginny was slow to rise, but that didn't stop Maddy. "I got no time to linger, girl."

Maddy was all business—and poetry in motion while she prepared their breakfast. "Chop the wood by six. Prep and start cookin' breakfast at seven. Coffee's goin', slicin' 'taters, and fryin' steaks, sometimes liver. By eight we're ringin' the bell and starts to servin'."

Maddy placed two skillets on the fire. Ginny walked over into the pie shack and sat down at a small table. "What'cha doin' dressed like a boy?" Ginny hesitated—too late. "A smart woman can do herself proud in this new country."

Pausing with two eggs in each hand, Maddy asked, "Ya know what's in these gold mines?" Not waiting for an answer, she cracked the eggs into the sizzling hot skillets. "Men! Toilin', desperate, down-hearted men goin' broke with their 'strikes it rich golden dreams'." Maddy, with a skillet in each hand, shuffled the eggs around and matter-of-factly flipped the frying eggs crisscrossing them into the opposite pan like a juggler and sat them back on the fire. "They creates their own hardships. I creates my own success."

Ginny watched Maddy's performance spellbound.

"These men are starved for want of tasty home cooking." Maddy grabbed the corners of her apron and held it out like a collection basket. "I means to fill this apron with gold, and yours too if you're willin' to string along. There's plenty to do."

Maddy added some chopped onions, peppers, and mix of spices to the skillets and dished up a couple plates for breakfast. She sat down with Ginny at the table.

Maddy was pleased Ginny put her hands together in prayer. "Dear Lord, thank you for watching out over Roscoe and me; for providing this meal; our new friend; and the aprons of gold we are about to receive. Amen."

Ginny took a bite and raved. "This is delicious!"

"I've been doin' this a long time." Maddy smiled and continued her story: "Miss, cookin's only the half of it. Before Mr. Lincoln took a stand and booted up, I was the house servant for the main house of a southern plantation—lived in the attic—I started in the wash house.

"Learned myself to read and write and cipher with nobody knowin' . . . listened to the master with my eyes wide open when he was talkin' business and investments with visitors and guests. I watched him barter, haggle, quibble—*ne-go-she-ate*.

"Seeing the Stars and Bars was on its last threads, master sent me around to collect stores for the mistress. That evening I asked the stableman to hook up the best field wagon with master's two best mules and have them ready to go early mornin'. I told him 'bout the conversation I overheard of the master talkin' 'bout splittin' up the man's family. I asked the stableman to ride along with me to pick up the stores.

"We left at first light. On the way we picked up

the man's family waitin' for us on Cross-Creek Road and kept on goin' 'til we were free."

Ginny was totally absorbed: "Maddy, you've done yourself real proud."

"Every step you take, child, should be towards a future of independence and self-worth."

Ginny pondered, reflecting on Maddy's words. "Independence." Just meeting this woman, Ginny appreciated her generosity and openness.

Maddy watched Ginny's reaction. "My first year cookin' with two iron skillets, I made twelve thousand dollars after expenses sellin' Maddy's pies."

Maddy took a forkful of eggs. "Eat up, child. We has work to do . . . And you know, I got a plan. I'm gonna grow my money—and buy land. That's how fortunes are made. Master taught me that."

7

APRONS OF GOLD

LIVING UNDERGROUND drilling rock, picking rock, blasting rock, timbering rock, mucking rock, and hauling rock with mules pulling ore carts out of the throats of mines, deep in the veins of the earth, was very dangerous work. The mines were widow makers.

With the little bit of money I was able to scrape together, I went mine to mine, crisscrossing Indian lands, a risky business, searching for Ginny and her family. Aiden and I took jobs in the Miss Pretty Mine.

I had just dumped a load of crushed rock and mine tailings. I was trailing a balky mule, pulling an empty ore cart back up the steep tracks about to enter into the Miss Pretty. The frayed hemp tow rope snapped, unleashing the cart. The heavy steel ore cart was on me in a flash—flipping me up, head over heals into the cart.

Racing down the rails, the cart was rollin', building up speed—clickety-clack—dropping faster and faster. Blurring past men and equipment the 'runaway' rattled, wobbling from side to side, screeching, sparking, squealing, and quickly running out of track.

The whole circus happened in a flash, but to me it was an eternity. At that raging speed, I thought, I'm a goner, sure—I'll be crashing through the Pearly Gates or racing into the flames of hell.

The shovel men and teamsters at the base of the mountain looked up gawking as my steel chariot left the earth, smashing through the railings at the end of the loading scaffolding. "Load in flight! Gangway!" I heard them shout. The shadow of the streaking cart struck their faces. In fear, they scrambled for their lives.

And then, silence. . . .

The cart launched upward and soared, hurling through the sky, rushing the life out of me on its way to my next divide . . . and, as in a dream, time stood still. The cart slowly turned a complete loop-de-loop in mid-air. Weightless, I felt I was about to turn inside out.

Falling back to earth, the cart plunged into the pile of crushed rock—BOOM! The report of the impact echoed, exploding like cannon fire striking its mark.

In a storm of dust, the miners rushed over to view my twisted corpse. They leaned in over my body, stiffly wedged and encased in the steel coffin.

Stunned and dazed I slowly opened my eyes as the dust cleared. Blurred by the blazing rays of sunlight, I looked up at the glaring eyes of dark, sweaty faces gawking and hovering over me.

Breathless, in shock, I asked, "Has my soul landed in Heaven or crashed in the devil's dust in hell?"

GINNY WATCHED as a wagonload of rough-sawn lumber passed by the pie shack. She was stacking kindling and prepping food. The teamster called out, "Save one of them pies for me, Ginny."

Ginny smiled, "I sure will, Loyal." As she watched the lumber wagon roll on over the bumpy road towards the mines, she had a thought. She hollered and ran after the wagon. "Will you sell me four long planks and a few 4 by 4 posts?"

"I don't see why not." The teamster jumped down from the work wagon. "Which ones do you want?"

"The two wide ones and those two narrow ones . . ." and, measuring with her hands to judge the width . . . "and five posts as well."

"What you building girl, a doll house?" Loyal laughed.

Ginny smiled, "How much do I owe you?"

"That's ok, Ginny, you only got a few boards."

"No, I don't want to be beholding to you. You buy my pies. I'll pay for your lumber. Will this cover it?"

Loyal smiled and took her money. "Yes, ma'am, it will. Thank you."

As he climbed back up on the wagon seat, Ginny said, "Thank you, Loyal. If you run into Bill Will or a carpenter, have him come around with his hammer and saw."

Ginny dragged the last of the four planks to the pile of lumber in the shade of the cottonwood tree.

She took a breath, swept her hair up into a pile on top of her head, grabbed a shovel, and started digging.

"My - my - my - my - my!" Maddy's voice always preceded her. "I leave you alone to your own devices and we's got new furniture." Maddy reined up the mules pulling her supply wagon to a stop and watched the goings on.

There, in the shade of the cottonwood tree, sat twenty miners benched-up, enjoying a sit-down supper on the new plank dining table, ten men per side. Ginny smiled and walked over to Maddy.

"Ginny, you done good! . . . I'm at a lost for words for what I'm seein' here!"

"Lost for words," Ginny laughed, "Oh, I'm sure you'll find them any moment."

"I'm proud of you girl."

"Plenty of new customers," smiled Ginny.

"Breakfast, noon, and supper—a dollar a pie!"

"Aprons of gold."

8

FLAMING ARROWS

AFTER A YEAR OF WORKING in the mines and wandering Indian Territory, I was lucky to be alive. I hadn't found Ginny and her family in the gold fields and they weren't in Wickenburg. I was on my way to Phoenix to look for her. It was late in the day as I rode along on a narrow Indian trail. I wasn't looking so good. Tired, worn out, used up, I was dying out there.

The trail down from the mine wove and meandered through the mountains where the clouds appeared close enough to reach out and touch. I was playing my mouth music, traveling through narrow outcroppings on both sides of the trail. Arrow, picking his way over slippery rock, balked and slowed. I thought it was on account of the rough terrain.

Boy, was I wrong.

I passed through a rock entrance into a small hidden clearing and came face to face with Indian boys with rifles and arrows pointed at all the important parts of me. I should have smelled their smoke. I had come upon their camp.

Facing off, they were a striking composite of feathers, beads, leather, and fur. I looked into the eyes of the closest Indian. He cocked his rifle. As I slowly turned my head, looking at each of their faces, I could see a lever cocking or an arrow being drawn back over a bow. I thought it best not to look at the last fellow, knowing that after the last hammer was cocked, there was only one thing left for them to do.

Taking my last breath . . . my eyes drifted back to the first brave. His rock-hard expression began to crumble. His eyes brightened and a broad smile lit up his face. He began to laugh, yes he did—they can laugh. He disengaged the hammer of his rifle and as he did, his brothers looked over at him in wonder. He pointed to a small trailside chain fruit cholla cactus. He made a motion as if he's holding one of the thorny fruits in his hand and touched it to different parts of his body, and then smiled, pointing to me.

Well, pretty soon the joke's on me. They all laughed and lowered their rifles and arrows. These were the very same Tonto Apache Indian boys who were going to ambush our wagons and had watched me crash into the giant cholla cactus. I was the boy who dances with pain.

The beef was on the fire and they fed me pretty good. We had few words in common but we were able to communicate well enough with hand gestures and drawings in the dirt.

They told me about Mother Earth and the Sun that rose and set on their land. And how their fathers' fathers' fathers hunted the buffalo on this land with bows and arrows, and now their days have changed from living to survival and being pressed from the West.

I felt their sorrow. My eyes found it hard to meet theirs. It was a moment of silence that held us all staring deep into the fire. . . . A pause of reflection that begged the question: Why is this boundless land of endless horizon not big enough for all the people? Are we not fingers on the same hand? . . .

I blew into my harmonica and we *were* back. They were fascinated by my mouth music. We sat around the fire. They grinned and laughed watching me puff and wiggle my fingers, cupping the shiny Hohner. Gesturing, I held it out to the leader, Blue Tail. Surprised, he backed off, waving his hands, 'no'. The others laughed and I laughed right along. Sitting closest to me, Loose Arrow decided he'd give it a go and extended his hand. I handed it to him. He held the harmonica carefully between his thumbs and forefingers. He slowly put it to his lips and blew. His breath screeched a piercing cord— startled, he dropped it like a hot potato. We all laughed and then passed the harmonica around the fire taking turns huffing and puffing out a melody.

Enjoying their company, I remembered the parting gift given to me by the pallbearers at my mock funeral, celebrating the blessed moment of my divine revival. The miners gave me a bottle of red-eye to warm me up on cold nights on the trail. And when things got rough, I might want to take a nip.

Well, we passed the bottle around. We were all about the same age, sixteen and seventeen—firing up. The music started to sound better, actually quite good for beginners. This was the first time I'd taken a drink and judging from what happened, it appeared it was their very first time as well. Pretty soon we were all laughing, acting silly, and dancing.

We watched the clouds in the sky tear themselves on the mountain peaks. They appeared to be closing in on us. The Indians picked up their bows and pierced the dried, fallen fruits of cholla cactus with their arrows and held them to the fire. Drawing back their flaming arrows, they shot them straight up into the night sky. Their arrows blazed upward, whistling with streaming fire, piercing the clouds. The clouds bloomed with fire and glowed with color.

Blue Tail handed me his bow and an arrow.

Gratified, I smiled and took my turn. It was quite an amazing sight to behold.

We did this over and over and shared our song into the night. . . .

The next morning at sunrise, four Indian boys and I stood at the edge of the largest cattle range I'd ever seen. Friends, we made our signs and said our goodbyes. As they rode off into the West, I'm pretty sure I heard them laughing.

Oh, what a night.

9

ABOUT TO CROW

JUST OFF THE HORIZON I gazed at the morning star, Venus. The palo verde trees and cactus flowers of springtime were abloom. I sat there on my Indian pony looking over the vast landscape and the colors of fire in the sky. My heart swelled and my eyes widened, feeling the grandeur before me. It was at that moment I realized even though I didn't know where I was going, I was not lost.

Enjoying the moment, I was surprised when I heard, "Howdy." Silently, a rider rode up alongside me. "Beautiful isn't it?" he commented, staring straight ahead.

"Yes. The Almighty used up all the good stuff when He created this. I was just about to crow."

The cowboy laughed.

Some men just look like cowboys—fit in the saddle, tall and lean, with an inner quality of strength and character measured beyond physical. I had just met that cowboy. "You lost?" he asked.

"No, sir. Just taking it all in."

"What are you doin' out here in the middle of God's country?"

"I don't know—passing through." Pausing, I said, "Thinking."

"Of where you've been or where you're goin'?"

"Both. The future mostly. What's done is done."

"The desert's a good place to be at sunrise, taking measure of oneself." And, as if measuring me, he said, "Destiny is a constant companion."

"I better watch out for tomorrow then, 'cause mine's off to a pretty shaky start."

Smiling he inquired, "Where are your folks?"

I pointed and looked up. "They left me early."

"Any family?"

"No. Almost."

Well, the cowboy and I talked for a spell. I told him about meeting and losing the love of my heart, "Like the sun, she made me shine," and about our abrupt parting on the trail. "I was left with this keepsake. I wear it in my pocket." Reaching into my shirt, I held up Ginny's pearl button for him to see.

Getting comfortable, we just sat there yakking as the sun greeted the day. I told him about my adventures. He especially liked the part about the devil's hogs from hell. "Yes sir, I was close enough to smell the smoke and feel the fire." He laughed. Then I got to laughing.

"You looking for work?" Taking a set in the saddle he said, "There's nothing like sunshine, the open range, and living the coarse, sparse life of a cowboy to clear your head and discover your mettle. You'll be good at it."

Smiling, I asked, "Why so?"

"You have spirit," he said, "I can see it in your heart." He broke into a broad smile. "Ride on up to the ranch house in Seven Springs and ask the old man if you can ride for his brand."

"Ranch house?"

The cowboy gestured like it was just over yonder.

I didn't see anything but miles of rocky, rolling hills, desert range, and cattle. I turned back, just about to ask him how to get there when he gestured, "Follow that peak. Good luck." With that, he picked up his reins and moved off . . . "And don't let the old man tell you he's full up. He's always got room for a good man."

"Thank you, sir. Say, who should I say sent me?"

Without turning, he answered, "Sunny. And be sure to give him my heartfelt hello." Riding away, Sunny asked, "What's your sweetheart's name?"

"Ginny. Ginny Hart."

I watched him turn into a shadow against the rising sun. His voice trailed off as he repeated, "Give him my heartfelt hello."

IT WAS A SHARP, CRISP SPRING MORNING in Black Canyon. Ginny, in a pretty cotton dress and apron, had been standing on a rock shelf catching the breeze and staring off into the distant mountain range.

"Hello, darlin'. Are you the pie lady?"

Ginny turned smiling, "Oh no. Maddy is the pie lady. I'm her apprentice."

"Well, you sure are pretty. I'd pay a dollar just to gaze on your smile," flirted the stranger with an Irish brogue, "I'm Aiden." He reached out to shake Ginny's hand. He held it more than long enough.

"Are you looking for something to eat?"

"Oh yes, ma'am."

Ginny stepped down off the rock shelf and walked over to the pie shack. "Fruit pie, vegetable pie, meat and potato pie, and mince pie. What would you like?"

"Meat with Irish potatoes if you have 'em, and something hot to wash it down with. I'm very hungry . . . Do you know if they are hiring at the mine?"

Ginny poured Aiden a cup of coffee. "They're always hiring. These mines are widow makers."

"Happens all the time. The last mine I was at—"

"What mine was that?" asked Ginny.

"The Miss Pretty, west of Wickenburg."

"I better make you two pies. What happened?"

"Just last week, a friend of mine, about my age, launched himself off the mountain in an ore cart."

"And was killed?"

"That's the thing! The cart sailed off the scaffolding, turned a complete loop-de-loop in midair and crashed, tumbling down the mountain."

. . . Ginny imagined the moment, "Is he dead?"

"We all thought he was a goner for sure, but when the dust cleared, WB got up, shook himself off, and walked away—"

"WB!—is he still at the mine!—Where is he? I have to find him!"

Aiden was surprised by Ginny's concern . . . his eyes widened, "Are you Ginny?"

Ginny nodded, "Yes, I am."

"He drew his wages and left. WB and I worked the mines side by side managing to avoid the 'crushes' and stay alive for over a year now and all he talked about was saving up enough money to find his Ginny."

"Where do you suppose he is now?"

Aiden shook his head, threw up his hands, and pointed off into the distance, "Somewhere out there . . . lookin' for you, darlin'."

10

THE OLD MAN

SO I STARTED OFF at a jiggle with an eye on the peak playing a tinny tune on my harmonica. I rode all day. And just as I started thinking I was lost, there was the ranch house.

I arrived just before sunset, passing a couple of roughs leaving through the gate as I was riding in. I heard them grousing, "That old crow couldn't tell a top hand from a fence post." Eyeing me, they snarled as they passed by, "Forget it, kid."

There was no missing the old man. A good hat covered his face. He was charging out of the ranch house as I rode up. A man framed-up tall of rough timber that with age had slumped and settled comfortably around the middle. He had a handsome face with a salted, grey mustache. His eyes were wise with a look of frontier hardship. I approached him with a, "Good day, sir."

He read me at a glance, "We're full up."

"There's always room for a good man, sir." He stopped in his tracks and then I said exactly what Sunny told me to say, "I'm looking to ride for your brand."

"You a cowboy?" he asked with a big booming voice.

"Not yet, sir," sounding like an unoiled hinge.

"Can you rope?"

"No, sir," shaking my head.

"Good with a knife?"

"No, sir," shaking my head.

"Do you have a knife?"

Shaking my head no.

"Shoe a horse?"

Shaking my head.

"Can you shoot?"

Still shaking my head.

"You handy with tools?"

Shaking no.

"Can you cook?"

Shaking no.

"You drink?"

"Just once, sir. I liked it."

His cold eyes measured me . . . "Well, you're not a liar. Praise the Lord. Boy, what can you do?"

Feeling lower than a snake, I reached into my pocket and pulled out my harmonica. "I'm workin' on my song."

Hard looking, he didn't laugh. Finished with me, he started walking off in a hurry, saying over his shoulder, "Sorry, son, but the outfit's full-handed. I just filled the last two bunks this morning."

Disappointed, I got back on Arrow, "Thank you for your time, sir." Turning to leave, I remembered what Sunny told me. I charged right over to the old man. Arrow stopped dead. I slid off, dropping the reins, "Sir," I caught the old man by surprise and gave him a big heartfelt hug. "Sir, Sunny told me when I see you I was to give you his heartfelt hello—'Hello.'"

Taken aback . . . the old man just gazed at me. "You met up with Sunny?" His eyes fixed on me. "How'd he look?"

"Yes, sir, he looked fine and fit on the range this morning."

The old man began to smile, a slow smile that started deep from inside and brightened his face.

Thinking that's that, I swung back up onto Arrow and turned to go. "Well, thank you, sir."

Raising his Stetson and running his hand through his hair he pointed, "The bunkhouse is over there. You can begin learnin' to be a cowboy by closing the gate. Earnin' your keep starts tomorrow at sunup."

I rode over and closed the gate.

"YOU AIN'T HERE NO MOR', Ginny, and you ain't happy." Ginny was moody. She slowly gathered up the dishes and forks into a basket on the plank dining table. "That young man you's always mooin' about has snatched your heart," said Maddy as she wiped the other end of the plank table . . . "And that's a natural thing."

"We only just met, Maddy, but he's the one, I know," said Ginny as she cleared the dishes.

"I've seen love and heartbreak that I couldn't do nothin' 'bout. But you're young and smart and nothin' or anythin' anybody says is gonna change your mind. And by the time you is as old as me, you'll realize that regret's the dearest price we pay. If you don't try to find your WB, you'll despair an' a big part of ya will wither away." Maddy stopped wiping and faced Ginny across the table.

Ginny put down the dishes. "I wake up in the middle of the night, all stirred up thinking the same thing."

"I ain't sayin' he's worth it. Men are tricky that way. He may be a snake all smilin' an' nice, turnin' your head an' twistin' ya up with song an' dance—romance. But only you can tell if he's gentle an' good—or a viper. Love's funny that way, once ya get bitten. . . ."

Maddy pulled a box tied with a string from her apron pocket.

"I got you a little something for your travels. Put it in your pocket for safe keepin' and don't tells nobody."

11

THE COOK

THE NEXT MORNING, I sat there in the dark waiting on the sun. I was about to learn that once you signed on, you stood by your pards and defended the outfit. If things didn't work out, you were free to drift. But until that time, you gave your word and you lived up to it. And that was that.

Being new, I wrangled the firewood, the water, and washed all the dishes. I loaded the chuck wagon's possum-belly with kindling, chunked the fires, greased the axles, harnessed the mules, and rode drag, choking in the dust. The days were hot, dry and long. When work needed to be done, I was at the head of the line.

Hatchet, the outfit's cook, had a thatch of silver-white hair and a disarming smile. He was recovering from a nasty spill and asked the old man for a helper on the cattle drive.

The old man obliged him, but said his cook's wages of two and a half dollars a day would be cut to a dollar and half per day. Hatchet said that would do. The old man was a businessman. He got two men for the price of one. He paid me with the dollar he saved on the cook.

Up before light, I built the cook fire and got the coffee going. I soon learned cooking for the outfit was more than boiling water. Mixing, flipping, rolling, frying, roasting, and smoking, Hatchet had it down. He could batch together a feast fit for kings. Mmmm, I still can taste his fancy fluff-duffs.

The old man had ranch chickens and a milk cow. He liked milk in his coffee. On roundups and drives, we traveled the chickens and left the cow at the ranch.

The cook was also the medicine man. For cuts, bruises, bites, gores, and toothaches, he had a variety of potions and lotions on board the 'cookie box.' That's what he called his chuck wagon.

"Keep lookin'. It's in there somewhere," shouted Hatchet. I was rooting around the shelves shuffling about the Epsom salts, calomel, kerosene oil, vinegar, arnica, salve, quinine, and mustang liniment—No whiskey was allowed on the trail.

"Try a drawer," pressed Hatchet.

In the first drawer I opened, I spied a tintype likeness of a handsome young couple dressed up in their frills and finest. I'm sure it was Hatchet and his lady. In all the time we rode together he never spent any words on her, but I often saw him gaze upon her in the light of the lantern, forlorn and missing her in the night.

Hatchet was tending to a cowboy sitting on a

cracker box with a terrible toothache. The boy was holding his swollen jaw, moaning in awful pain. "Think about swishing around some water after meals, boy. A little vinegar water once in awhile, would be a good idea," advised the doc.

"Found 'em!" Hatchet had a pair of steel pliers, angled and filed down for pulling rotten teeth.

Muffled in throbbing pain, the patient mumbled, "Ya can yank 'em all doc if 'n it'll stop the pain."

Yes sir, Hatchet was the watch that kept things ticking. With his good nature and reputation for tasty vittles, the outfit was never short handed. He was the reason many of them hired on.

On drives, I was up in the morning at three, working around the fire and stiff sleeping cowboys, some who had just gotten' off night watch and would be up at quarter past five to gobble breakfast.

The glow of a lantern would light up the chuck wagon. Hatchet was in the habit of talking to himself as he cooked. "With a cup of flour, a pinch of this, a dab of that—Helper, put two Dutch ovens on the coals." Visualizing the quantity needed and the measurements of the ingredients, he unconsciously calculated with his thumb and his fingers, "Three, four, six, seven. . . ."

While preparing one dish, he would have me working on another. "Helper, grab up sixteen potatoes, cut out the dark spots and chop 'em up fine," and he'd be right back to his fixin's. "With just the right amount of shortening and half a pour of what's in this bottle—"

"What's in that bottle?" I asked.

Hatchet just smiled not about to divulge Merlin's

secret potion. "Crack open eight eggs, and whip 'em in a bowl." He taught me how to make a dandy boggy-top—a pie washed down with a hot cup of Arbuckles', leaving the cowboys wanting more.

Breakfast was a commotion of cowboys and wranglers coming and going; gobbling down chuck; packing up gear; loading the chuck wagon and riding out to drive the herd. And all the while Hatchet made it look easy.

Right after breakfast we flapped the reins and rolled the mules out. Seeing a cowboy's war bag and hot roll still spread out on the ground, I was about to jump off the wagon and load it on. Hatchet stopped me and said, "Leave it. It ain't that waddy's first time." We hurried on so we could set up for the noon meal and rendezvous with the outfit half way up the trail.

Gathering, rounding up, and pushing a string of two thousand head of wild-eyed and spooky cattle up the trail while riding green broncs, was a dangerous stunt. With thrashing tails, bobbing horns, and tramping hooves, the sudden sound of a hack or cough or flighty shadow could set the herd off into a frenzy—a cowboy's nightmare—Stampede!

The heaving mass of cattle kicked up an endless rolling cloud of dust as they snailed along ten to fifteen miles before nightfall.

Road runners darted and raced alongside the wheels of the chuck. I looked over the open range at the distant horizon. In the lead, it was our job to scout for water, find a campground, and be prepared to greet the outfit with a hot meal for supper.

Hatchet reminded me of the captain of a ship.

A pilot with a good sense of direction, he had a compass in his head.

We hardly ever butchered our own cattle, usually it was another man's brand. It didn't matter none, he butchered one of ours right back, so it all evened up. Or, we would hunt game. Riding along looking off over the range, Hatchet reined up the mules, Sally and Rocky. "Hand me the rifle." I handed him the 'Trapdoor,' Springfield. "See it there, up on the rocks?"

I looked out in the direction of Hatchet's gaze. A mule deer, way off in the distance was standing in the shade of the mesquites. "Good eye, sir, but it's too far off."

From the seat of the wagon Hatchet drew up slowly, adjusted the sights, taking careful aim. "Take a breath . . . aaand squeeze. . . ." Through a cloud of smoke, I watched the deer.

"Missed," I said.

"Not yet. . . ."

A moment later the buck dropped in its tracks.

"Fire in the morning, lands in the afternoon," smiled Hatchet.

"That's one fine shot, sir."

"Meat tonight! Cowboys' delight."

Hatchet didn't say much. He banked his words and saved them for when they counted. "That's our spot up ahead. Water—a cocktail for a thirsty herd, good grazing, plenty of firewood, and we'll be out of the way."

All day we had been zigzagging up, down and all around. I looked over the immeasurable vastness of the open range. "You sure they'll find us?"

"Oh, I'm pretty sure they'll find us, alright. Between the water and our smoke, they'll just follow their noses. I haven't lost a herd yet." He rolled the wagon up to a stop. "Take this sixty-footer." He handed me a *reata*, "Loop it around that dead stump, stretch it out and fasten a stick to the other end. And, scribe me a circle in the dirt."

With that done, Hatchet positioned the cookie box in the center of the circle and matter-of-factly told me, "Your last chore tonight is when the stars come out, be sure to point the tongue of the wagon in the direction of the North Star so the old man will have a sense for which way to head the cattle out in the morning. Don't forget."

Everything was matter-of-fact and easy with Hatchet, until you forgot—I didn't forget. How could I? Every night when I pointed the wagon towards the North Star, I thought of Ginny. I enjoyed the last chore of the day and remembered her breath on my ear as she whispered a secret. "*I love you.*"

I unhitched the mules, lowered the flapboard, and set up the poles to stretch the chuck's canvas fly for shade and we got to cooking. I was hungry.

"Wrangle up some water, enough for drinkin' now and coffee in the morning. By the time them cows top off tonight, that water will be beef tea and plenty tough."

The Dutch ovens were on the coals and the venison was slowly roasting. Over a cup of coffee Hatchet made his joke, "What's WB stand for? . . . White Beans?" Smiling, from one cook to another I enjoyed his company and his recipe.

My job was to keep the stew from boiling and

turn and baste the roast. "Slather that good sauce all over."

Then Hatchet unveiled 'the crock.' "The secret to sourdough is in the age of the starter." My mouth watered. He guarded that crock of starter like it was family. And, with reflective pause . . . "This starter was passed on to me at Gettysburg from a cook whose grandfather scavenged it from a fleeing British regiment on the run in 1776—yeast, flour, sugar, and potato water to feed the fermenting yeast—this is alive and requires a watchful eye. Never use all of it and always replace what you use."

While rolling balls of soft dough in the palms of his hands, Hatchet shared some trailside wisdom which he was prone to do from time to time. "We got new hands on this drive and they can do, and be, whatever they want out there. But within this kitchen circle, they'll mind their manners."

Sure enough, late in the afternoon, we could see the rising canopy of dust from the cattle. Smelling the water, the bellowing herd was coming on.

Hungry from the tasty aromas of the baking, boiling, and sizzlin' fixin's, I was ready to eat the smoke.

The cattle were all watered and grazing. It was time for supper. "Get ready, White Beans," said Hatchet. "Here comes hungry."

Well, right off, blazin' in, I could see it coming. The race was on. Two cowhands, Eddy and Barlow, were dashin' and splashin' in for grub. I looked over at the cook, he was on simmer. The two breezed into the circle dragging dust. We watched as their dust floated over the Dutch ovens, stew pots, and the roast. They tied off their horses to the wheels of the chuck wagon and stepped to the head of the line.

You don't argue with a mule, play with skunks, or start something with the cook.

Hatchet stepped forward with a smile, "What can I do for you, boys?"

"We's hungry dawgs! Ooow! Ooow! Ooo—"

And before they could finish their howl, the cook comes to a boil, rapping on their chests with the big kettle spoon, backing them down and out of the circle. "You stampede into my chuck, dusting my ovens and pots, glazing my fine roast with dirt! Have you no manners?"

The boys sputtered and stuttered.

Shaking the spoon, he pointed down to the line in the dirt circling his empire and said, "Don't cross that line without asking my permission first. In the future, and that means right now, before you ask for that privilege, think about rubbin' up, dust yourselves off, wash your hands and face and rake your hair before you come up to dine at my banquet table . . . and furthermore, the next time you blaze on in here and tie off your horse to the wheel of my chuck, I'm cookin' it."

Watching from a safe distance, the whole outfit stood off, glad it wasn't them facing up to the spoon. His point made, and knowing he had the full choir's attention, Hatchet turned to the outfit, "And, one more thing. If you waddies want to sleep in your hot roll tonight, make sure you roll it up in the morning and stuff it into the wagon. It's a long ride back."

That was the law . . . and order.

12

"DON'T BE SHY, GIRL"

IT WAS A LONG RIDE. Ginny was trail-worn and determined to find WB. She was dressed well and had a new saddle on Roscoe. She wore a western hat and thought it best to dress as a man for her personal safety. Virgil was military and taught his daughter well. She sat a mule or a horse as good as any rider.

She had done well under Maddy's tutelage. Maddy said she would invest Ginny's share of the profits in land right alongside hers in California. Ginny had enough money to spend and travel by stagecoach if she wanted, but Aiden said WB was headed cross-country towards Phoenix on horseback and the stage would slow her search.

It was late afternoon when she and Roscoe picked up the trampled trail of the herd. The canopy of trail dust was still settling and aglow in the long golden rays of the sun. The western landscape was gorged with molten color.

Watching the birds fly overhead Ginny was confident she would find water. In two hours it would be dark. Roscoe caught the scent and picked up the pace. He didn't stop until he was standing in a waterhole surrounded by long green grass.

Ginny set up camp and gathered some sparse pieces of wood and started a small cook fire. Waiting on the fire to turn to coals, Ginny climbed out of her clothes and slipped into the refreshing waterhole. Roscoe munched on the tall grass.

She swam and splashed as the sun set and the reflection of the moon appeared in the water, reminding her of WB's promise, *"I will love only you all the days of my life."*

Roscoe brayed—but it was too late. "Well, ain't y'all a purty little fish." Ginny sank into the water up to her chin. "Don't be shy, girl. I'll be right in to join ya," said Eddy the young cowboy with the billy goat beard as he climbed down off his horse.

"Stay right there. I don't want your company!"

The cowboy started taking off his shirt. "I'll wash yur back an y'all can wash mine."

"Mine's already washed and I'm particular about the fish I swim with."

The cowboy smiled and kicked off his boots. Ginny glanced around looking for a route of escape. "Skinny dippin's a ho' lot a fun once ya gets usta it."

"Is that what yur sister said?" snapped Ginny.

"Yur a mouthy one, arn'ch ya, missy."

The cowboy lunged into the water and Ginny quickly made her way over to the tall grass and dodged behind Roscoe. Eddy splashed around thinking she was underwater.

Ginny put her shirt on and quickly buttoned her pants. Looking around, Eddy saw Ginny had him at a disadvantage.

Ginny was standing at the edge of the water pointing Eddy's six-shooter at him.

"Now girl, ya ought not to be doin' that. I wuz just funin'."

Ginny cocked the pistol, "Well, in case you didn't notice, I wasn't having any fun." Aiming the gun at Eddy, Ginny said, "You lie to me and you'll be coloring the water . . . Understand?" He shook his head 'yes'. "What's your name?"

"Eddy."

"What are you doin' here, Eddy?"

"I come back fur my bedroll. Furgot ta load it on the wagon this mornin' when the outfit rolled out."

"Tough luck for you. Is there someone in the outfit calls himself WB?"

"Why? What'd he do to you?"

Ginny took a step and better aim at Eddy.

Eddy paused to think . . . he was a good liar. "WB wuz with the outfit, but he fell off his horse and wuz dragged, cracked his head on the rocks—"

"When? Where'd this happen?"

"Week ago, maybe mor."

"And, you left him there!" exclaimed Ginny.

"What's we spost-ta' do? A herd of two thousan' cows don't wait fur one cowboy. It's jus' his hard luck."

Ginny gathered up Eddy's clothes and threw them to him. "Put these on." She picked up his boots. "And these, too," tossing them in as well. As he dressed, Ginny quickly put her boots on and said, "Bet you're so mad you could spit, huh?"

Eddy splashed and flopped around in the water getting dressed. Ginny asked, "Where is it?"

"Where's whut?"

"Your bedroll."

"Over there, other side the wash."

"You better be telling the truth. And don't shoot yourself in the foot."

"Not my—" Eddy's six-shooter splashed into the waterhole.

Ginny walked over to the wash. Sure enough there was the sleeping roll and his saddlebags. The wagon tracks were headed north. Ginny heard the sound of the six-shooter cocking and turned to face Eddy. "It's yur turn ta' dance, missy." Eddy was a sight all dripping and grinning.

Ginny gave Eddy his moment. "You're a real . . . desperado, Eddy," and then she took a step forward opening her hand to reveal six bullets. And with a little more lean towards Eddy, she had his full attention. Eddy's face went fright as he slowly looked down at the palm derringer.

Ginny pressed the barrel into his wet shirt. "You best get on your horse and ride back to your outfit before I decide 'it's jus' yur hard luck.' "

Eddy holstered his six-shooter and picked up his gear. "Yur a tough one, missy."

"Pray you don't meet my father."

13

ROCKIN' AND ROASTIN'

ISIDORO, A SPANISH CALIFORNIO and older than the rest of the outfit, was reduced to his present state of chasing cows as a result of his fascination, persistence, and passion—an unquenchable love of gambling ran in his blood. When his aristocratic family's empire crumbled, he lost the inheritance of the lordly land holdings given to them by the King of Spain in the sixteenth century.

Isidoro would gamble at the drop of the dice, or games of cards—faro, monte, chusa, and poker. He loved cockfights, bullfights, horse racing—the lottery. Or in lazier moments, he would wager if a frog would leap once . . . twice . . . or three times.

He would gamble on or for anything except the gold *caballo* charm hanging on the gold chain around his bronze neck and the silver inlaid sky stone—the turquoise bracelet his grandfather had traded for Mexican parrot feathers. The bracelet never left his wrist.

Win or lose it appeared to make little difference to him. He was as gallant at losing as everything else he took up.

His horsemanship had no equal. He was the first to dash into a tangle of mesquite, raking leather —chancing a blind eye poppin' snaky cattle.

The breed of our camp was a full measure less than the ancestral heritage of Isidoro. Being that none of the boys had ever opened the door to a schoolhouse, when he told a story around the campfire, we were all ears. Isidoro could remember a story like it was book-read—he was, 'El Book'.

With good English and the flair of a Spanish accent, he told of romantic memories and passionate stories passed down through the generations of the *caballeros* and *vaqueros* of his family.

El Book knew horses.

"*Amigos! Muchachos!* Buckaroos! What I tell you is true. *Dios* created the *caballo*—the horse—magnificent spirited animals of beauty, grace, and speed—royal mounts fit for the pleasures of kings and queens.

"Charles V, Holy Roman Emperor, King of Spain, looking to expand his empire, and with rumors of gold and riches in the new world, dispatched an armada of sailing ships, heavy with guns and huge white canvas sails that rose to capture the high winds and imaginations of early explorers.

"Daring to cross the endless horizon of crashing waves and bottomless ocean, *Hernán Cortés*, with sixteen *caballos* on board—very fine they looked—landed his eleven Spanish ships in Vera Cruz in 1519. They were the first horse tracks on the new world.

Born with passion, his story was mesmerizing.

"*Cortés* harbored his ships and anchored offshore. Then he and his men waited for the moonlight. They crossed the water riding the swimming horses ashore. They were armed with sticks that thundered and fired lightning. The Indians had never seen a horse or firearms before and were frightened thinking these intruders—men upon horses—were beasts from the sea with two heads and six legs.

"The Indians fled into the jungle. And in the days that followed, they watched from the shadows as the intruders burned their own ships in a great blaze."

Captivated by his performance, our ears were sponges, our eyes bugged out, and our jaws went slack.

"Their medicine men were not able to ward off this evil magic." With lyrical gestures, El Book shuffled around the fire stirring up the flames, "All their dancing and singing and all their smoke did not stop the ships from arriving with more horses.

"As time went on, these eleven stallions and five mares, Arabian barbs, strayed, wandered and bred with the other horses forming small bands. These spirited horses survived in spite of the short mountain grasses and semi-arid climate. They became the stunted and sturdy wild mustangs we ride today.

"Huge numbers of *vacada*—cattle—bred and endured much like the *caballo*. Roaming the plains and ranges for centuries, they multiplied becoming wild—as wild as deer. These Spanish longhorn cattle arrived in 1521 and so did the *vaqueros*—or as you call them, cowboys."

After three months of pushin' cows and choking trail dust, we were back at the ranch. I was helping Hatchet, who appeared to be fully recovered from his accident, move supplies into the cook shack.

The old man didn't miss much, "WB, leave that load to Hatchet, he's milked it 'bout long enough. He's going to want a maid tomorrow."

"An' a butler," quipped Hatchet.

I put down the box of Arbuckles' coffee and caught up to the old man on his way to the ranch house.

Hatchet called out, "I'll thank you for my dollar a day in wages back, sir."

"Yeah, yeah, yeah," bristled the old man.

The old man always walked like he was on a mission. Turning to me, "It's time to get you on a horse."

I'd never been to the ranch house. Hands stayed in the bunkhouse where we slept, ate, played cards, and stored our stuff—whatever we had, and it wasn't much. So when the old man asked me up to the ranch house, I was pretty excited.

"Come on in."

It was the first house I'd been in in three years. The ranch house had real glass windows cut into the adobe walls. Large round peeled timbers supported the ceiling of planks. The hearth was set in the center of a stacked stone fireplace. There were colorful Indian rugs on the floor. A collection of rifles and carbines, Sharps and Spencers, hung on racks along the walls. "Nice house, sir."

The old man went over to a fine, tall cabinet, rummaged around and pulled out a pair of rusty spurs and a knife. "You'll need these."

Looking around, just making conversation, "Sir, have you ever had a notion of doing something other than cowboying?" I had opened a heavy door.

Lifting his eyes, the old man pulled back the spurs. "Son, cowboying is my way of life, the way I live. This is my home, my land, fought and paid for. I live free and fair—my terms, my business."

Looking eye to eye, standing toe to toe for what was to be the longest, most awkward moment of my life, the old man was not finished.

"Cowboying is the hardest, toughest, hottest, coldest, dustiest, wettest, dangerous, and most thrilling work I've ever done. And if you're expecting anything different, then you best not put these on."

Sharp as flint, the old man had a way with words and I didn't miss one of them. He expected an answer and he waited for it. Stumped up, I searched for a reply. I looked down at the spurs in his hand. After a long, long moment, "Sir, I think they'll fit."

Sitting around the campfire, the outfit made their charge. "WB, ya lookin' ta trade the shade of the chuck's fly fo' forkin' horses—rockin' and roastin' in the hot sun?" asked Eddy snidely, now smoldering with his own personal axe to grind.

No longer the cook's helper, I was their fair game. Lifting an eye from my plate, looking over the fire and around the circle, I could feel thunder rolling in. The vaqueros and cowboys were sizing up the new button. Eddy slowly drawled, "Brandin' cattle's a ho' lot different than bakin' biscuits, Sovereign. Ya best think 'bout it fo' ya climbs aboard. Cuz if y'all don't cuts it, it's git-git-git alooong lil' doggie, you're on your—"

"Way home! Blaaah!" bawled Barlow who always echoed Eddy's voice and finished his song.

"Th' tenderfoot 'll be trail boss by th' end of th' day!" jested Eddy.

"Trail boss by th' end of th' day," laughed Barlow from his mouth of decay.

Wiping out a dish and not looking over at the prattlers, Hatchet cooled the boiling pot, "I'll be wagerin' on WB's grit over your blow."

Had the boys not favored my cooking, it would have been full-out laughter. As it was, they just winked around and snickered.

Restless, I awakened early the next morning, anxious to get started and ate with Hatchet. Lifting a fork, the cook served up his recipe, "Just stay on your horse."

"That's it?"

"Pretty much. If you have it in you, you'll find it. And, if you don't, they'll see it."

Scraping my plate clean, I laughed, "Stay on my horse?"

"Yep."

I put my dishes in the wash tub, mounted up, and rode out alone, easing into the darkness.

In the solitude of the morning, admiring the majesty of the sunlit haze rising on the snowcapped peaks of the purple mountains, I was filled by the awesome power of a sunrise glowing over the fertile range, running free from the horizon in all directions.

The Indian embraced Mother Earth, realizing their oneness of spirit from their very beginning. I was feeling that spirit and discovering my dream. And before I grew old, I would experience both.

I joined the round-up of wild range cattle scattered and hidden in the arroyos and ridges of the distant landscape. My joy and observation were harshly interrupted by assaults to my nature dealt daily by stiff company. The cutlery of their barbs and biting jest belittled and made me feel the fool.

Apparently Eddy's thirty mile round-about retrieving his forgotten bedroll gave him time enough to grow dislike for the cook and now harvest his revenge on the cook's helper.

It got rough fast.

Once after dinner, I was mounted up waiting on the outfit. Without me noticing, Barlow snuck around and put a prickly pear fruit under Arrow's tail. His immediate performance made for the mid-day amusement and pleasure of the outfit. Arrow went to pitching and bucking and hopping around the camp, stomping on the fire, scattering the hands, flipping over the coffee pot and pans, tearing down the fly on the chuck wagon, and flap-jacking me into the wild blue yonder.

Eddy was well liked, with a quick lip. He inspired the cowhands' relentless parade of insults and sport with me. Whatever I did or had to say, fell on deaf ears or was fodder for ridicule. With tone and temper, they made me feel small.

Grey skies and muddy water came over me, shaping my thinking. My temper ran afoul. I slipped into melancholy and turned inward. I was alone.

Long days were followed by longer nights. Riding night watch on wild cattle we were readying to sort-out and trail brand, I heard Eddy run his mouth and the laughter of the hands around the campfire.

In the habit of making unexpected visits, the old man silently rode up beside me circling the herd, "Beautiful night."

"Yes, sir, it truly is."

"Doing more than your share of night guard?"

"Better than feeding the cackle around the fire." I was ready to rip.

"Kind'a sour are ya?"

"Sir, I'm looked upon as an empty vessel, not fit to hold reins, barely able to ride the wood!"

The old man answered me as if he hadn't captured my mood. "I see you stopped kickin' your horse . . . your riding is improving. You're stayin' in the middle. There's drape in your reins . . . you're feelin' it—developing a light touch. In time it'll all come together, boy."

Like I said, the old man didn't miss much.

"Thank you, sir."

"The boys you're riding with have those skills, son. Had 'em since they were bitty. Vaqueros were held in the arms of their papas and rocked to sleep while riding the rhythm of a walking horse. Cowboys were whirling and dropping their strings on the rooster while collecting eggs for momma."

Turning to me with a smile, he continued, "They're not about to let a greenhorn ride with the outfit without tuning him up." He paused, "It's time to come out of the shade, boy. Force and resistance are the same thing. If you got it, give it."

Letting his words set in, he told me, "Go on and get some rest. You're going to need it in the morning. I'll take the watch."

Chewing on the old man's words, I was put off. Just about to say something, I bit my lip and drifted off leaving the old man watching my back. "Night, sir."

Mulling over his words, I rode back to camp, jumped into my bag and went to sleep.

The corrals were a swirling chaos of colors and 'loco' motion with hair-raising hides, powerful hooves, and whirling sharp horns in a constant trumpet of lowing, blatting, snorting, and bellowing.

I plunged in with all the enthusiasm of an empty sack, worried this would be the end of me.

Blinded by the smothering dust, smoke, and sweat, the perils of working on foot and being gored, bit, kicked, and stomped went on day after day.

We roped and tossed animals struggling to bust free, bawling in pain from our branding irons and ear marks in what appeared to me to be Lucifer's playground.

And yet, day after day, there were not a scrappier lot of good-humored pranksters—mostly at my expense. More than one time, while I waited by the fire to drop the next calf, all the loops of every cowhand's lariat found me, laying me out to roll in the dust of their laughter. Their rough company did not crease or fold me. Try as they may, I did not buck. If they scratched for a weakness, my hide stayed intact.

I had ignored Eddy's increasing assaults to my humor in attempt to provoke me.

It was late in the day and the hands were spent. The smells of supper wafted over and mixed with the stale, singed stench of branding. Barlow was picking up and I was pulling the irons from the hot coals of the branding fire.

The corrals were near empty. Wild with room to run, the few remaining steers were hostile, nervous, and threatening.

All day in the sweltering heat, Eddy had been needling, "Columbus! Ya'll b' careful of those tender, lovin' hands of yurs with them hot, heavy, heavy irons."

A line of punchers clearing the corrals yelled and fanned their hats moving the ornery steers back out to the open range.

Eddy was working over the branding chute, a narrow passage of poles and rails that ran alongside the corral allowing twenty cattle, head-to-tail, to enter at a time. Eddy kept gnawing at me with his jaw-flappin' lip. "What's I got t' do t' release yur wolf —so's I can skin yur hide? Brand yur 'sweet-tart's' pearly button to yur forehead?"

"Ooow," howled Barlow mouthing his base nature, "Sweet-tart."

Enough's enough, "Eddy, why don't ya'll bring that hot mouth of yurs over here and I'll brand it up nice an' purdy fur' ya! And, I'll clip yur ears back."

Cracking his knuckles, "Ti yi yo, be right over, dogie." With a gust of wind, Eddy's hat flipped off and sailed into the chute. He jumped down to retrieve it.

It happened in a tick. A savage bull whirled, breaking back through the line of arm-wavers, scattering the punchers and stormed into the open end of the chute.

Startled and penned-in, Eddy saw the raging bull. Terror gripped his face. He glanced wide-eyed over at me through the rails.

I watched the chute rumble and shake. Racking from side to side, the furious bull charged Eddy. With flaring nostrils, the bull lowered his head for ram.

Struck by the action, I grabbed up a smoldering branch of firewood and wheeled, thrusting it into the chute across the poles just as the horns of the bull's head slammed into it, ripping it from my hands, snapping it like a matchstick, showering Eddy with sparks.

The chute creaked, shuttering dust end-to-end. I winced and the cowhands gasped, as the log splintered, but held just inches from a shaking Eddy. A hanging ember sparked, singeing Eddy's billy-goat beard. Dazed, the bull bellowed releasing his slobbering drool, spraying Eddy.

Eddy didn't rush to thank me, but the slings and arrows stopped. And a new rawhide, worthy of the outfit with a nature they could depend on, joined the fire and laughter of their circle.

THE BLACK BIRDS of death made wide circles in the sky.

Ginny had been riding towards the birds, anticipating finding the remains of life—WB's.

Turkey vultures are cleaners—buzzards. They are scavengers that scour the desert and pick the bones of all living things unfortunate enough to die. Vultures are a smelly lot, but very good at their task.

Eddy had told Ginny that WB had fallen and was badly injured. Could these vultures be waiting for WB to pass? She spurred Roscoe to make him go faster but it was hot and he had one speed—slow.

When Ginny had first seen the birds, their circles were high and wide. Now they were lower and spiraling in. She encouraged Roscoe to move. "Water, Roscoe! Water!" His ears pricked up and even though he didn't smell water, he obeyed Ginny and picked up the pace.

As she approached the grounds of death, she could see one mule down. He was dead.

For a moment Ginny thought of her parents.

An ox stood yoked—motionless in the blazing sun. Ginny rode in fast, circling the collapsed wagon to scare off the buzzards. One red-headed buzzard was already ripping at the dead man who was crushed under the wheel of the fallen wagon.

The buzzard floundered and flapped off.

The man's wife was blindly waving a broom into the sky. She was in a state of delirium and couldn't tell the difference between the real birds and the ones she imagined.

Ginny tried to calm the raving woman, but the woman struggled and struck out at her. Ginny decided to let her be.

Ginny didn't know if it was her imagination or

if something moved under the wagon. Dusty and huddled down in the tilt of the fallen wagon, crouched a small boy of seven or eight staring beyond Ginny with a blank look—a ghostly look—she had seen it before. The boy was parched and just on this side of being frightened to death.

Ginny quickly got her canteen of water. She found a cloth in their empty wagon and tore off two squares. She soaked them with water and crawled back under the wagon. She placed one cloth around the boy's neck. He was too dry to drink, but if he could slowly suck water from the cloth maybe he would not die. Ginny held it gently to his lips. After a long while his eyes blinked and he opened his lips. He touched his tongue to the wet cloth.

Slowly he began to suck water. Ginny rewet the cloths many times while she looked about deciding what to do next.

The boy's mother had waved her broom until she collapsed and fell dead swatting at the black-winged shadows on the ground. Ginny dragged her over next to her husband and covered them both with the wagon's canvas.

The dazed boy was now able to sip water. Ginny led him away from the wagon and his ripe Pa and sat with him in the shade of a mesquite tree.

"We used the last of our water, Roscoe. And without it, we'll die. No time to bury them. We're leaving here tonight—it'll be cooler," said Ginny as she unyoked the ox. "We'll go as soon as the boy is strong enough to ride old Brandywine here. Roscoe, you make him go."

It was twilight and the moon was rising full.

The ox and Roscoe moved side by side at a good pace. The boy was alert and appeared to enjoy riding the ox. "Where are we going?"

Ginny smiled. These were the boy's first words. "What's your name," asked Ginny.

"Twig . . . Where are my folks?"

"Your pa's fixing the wagon. They'll be along."

It was a beautiful night and they were making good time, but Ginny looked worried. Roscoe smelled the smoke and Ginny saw the blazing campfire. At first she thought it was an Indian fire. "That fire is much too big for an Indian fire. It must be a wagon train of proud huckleberries advertising for company."

As they got closer, Ginny and Twig could hear the fiddle and able to count the wagons. It was a train of fifteen circled up.

Ginny and Twig rode right up close before the fiddle stopped, the dancers turned, and the men and children noticed the ox, mule, and two riders watching them from between the wagons.

Their presence was a shocking surprise to the settlers . . . one of the little boys broke the silence when he recognized and shouted: "Twig!"

Looking around the camp, Ginny said, "We saw your bonfire clear across the valley. And so could Geronimo if he was out there—where is your night guard? Can you men imagine the thrill and excitement your women would have dancing the *Virginia reel* with Apache warriors?"

14

COWBOYING

STANDING IN THE SHADOWS of the vaqueros, I had kept my ears cocked. I thought it best to model my performance. My eyes drank in everything. I watched the knacks of the wranglers and the ways of the cowboys. Up before the sun and last in the saddle at night, I worked hard and learned fast, honing my skills. I learned where to be and when to be there.

I picked up Spanish pretty good listening to El Book's stories: "The shoes on my grandfather's horses were made of silver."

Roping was an art. The vaqueros were masters. They could rope a snake. Coordinating distance with the speed and running power of a steer with the speed of your horse required perfect timing.

I learned to whirl a sixty foot *reata*—rope.

Galloping full-out, pitching a long cast, placing the *lazo*—loop, under the steer's feet at the exact moment they came off the ground, and with the catch—set up my horse for the shock while taking the slack out of the rope and wrapping a couple quick dallies around the saddle horn without losing a finger or thumb, took practice. I got good at it.

Got so when I loosened the thong and shook out a loop, my horse knew we were going to the dance. Maintaining position, avoiding a side pull, and facing the animal, he kept a constant tug.

The old man took his time, showing me the how-to-dos. He put a real brainy cutter in my string. The cutter made me look good. When a steer had to be cut from the herd for any reason—branding, sale or doctoring—we'd start slow and easy, quietly urging the steer to the outside of the herd. And with a sudden dash, the steer was separated. When the steer tried to rejoin the herd, my horse anticipated his every move. With speed and action, we could spin and turn faster than the steer.

The old man taught me how to shoot and he showed me how to hunt.

I remember the first time I fired a shotgun. We were out along the piñon pines. He was anxious to try out two brand-new, out-of-the-crate, Remington and Sons double barrel 10 gauge. Keeping the wind on our side, I got so I could drop game with every pop.

Riding back to the ranch house, we enjoyed the rewards of the day—wild turkeys swung over the backs of our saddles. Looking down, I noticed the rusty spurs he had given me had polished up to a nice shiny patina.

It had been a while, and I was keeping an eye out for Sunny. One day I reined up alongside the jigger boss and asked, "Say, boss, when will Sunny be comin' in?"

He replied, "You seen 'im too?"

"Yeah. I wanted to thank him for hookin' me up with the outfit."

He told me that Sunny was jigger boss before he got the job, and that Sunny was the old man's son. One day Sunny's ridin' point on a herd to market when somethin' spooked 'em. They got to rollin' quick. When the dust cleared, Sunny was gone. His passin' left the old man heartbroken.

"But, I saw Sunny, real as you and me sittin' here."

"On a Spanish mustang, dappled white with patches of gray and black?"

"Yep, that very one."

"Used to be on reports of seein' Sunny, and raisin' the old man's hopes, we would ride out to search for him. After a while we just gave that up." As we both looked out over the range, he continued, "Oh, Sunny's out there, alright. Rimmin' around, ridin' on ridge tops and the high points, lookin' for strays."

He clucked, jingled his spur, and rode off. We never spoke of it again.

Without really knowing, I had built a reputation. Wasn't long before the old man gave me a chance to boss a greasy sack outfit—brush-poppin' for cattle and scouring for mustangs in rough country.

Terrain too rough for wagons, we ran our food and supplies in on mules and horses.

Every day was a challenge. Rounding up mustangs, I admired their wild freedom. Elusive and smart, they would run for days requiring our persistence and patience. Breaking them, I learned to fly. My landings needed work. Loose and limber, I learned to roll.

In all the years of cowboying, the hardest thing for me or any other cowboy was to ride his string of horses up the trail and have them sold along with the cattle on delivery.

With the herd sold and wearing three months of trail dust and stink, the outfit scrubbed up ready to let loose. We were having a soak and splashing about in a waterhole—all naked or half naked— washing our backs and our horses. Our clothes, all faded, worn out, and torn, weren't worth washing. The dry goods store would be my first stop in town.

A photographer in a black high-top wagon drove out from town, arriving during our bath. The gentleman addressed us, asking if we would like our photographs taken and our likeness recorded for posterity. All lathered up, one of the hands told him we didn't have any photographs, and asked, "Who's posterity?"

"Gentlemen, allow me to demonstrate." The photographer started explaining about photography and set up a little black box with a lens on a wood tripod. "Gentleman, please observe. This is a true remembrance—a souvenir for all time."

When I looked through the lens, I could see whatever I pointed it at, but it was upside down and real small.

The photographer was a magician with grand arm-waving gestures and lingo beyond the stars. "Gentlemen, when the light passes through the lens into the camera," he paused knowing his customer. "It brands!—brands an image onto a piece of glass. And hocus-pocus—it makes a picture."

Zack, with his head full of soapsuds, spoke up. "Mister, can you chew that hocus-pocus a little finer?"

The boys saw no real value and expressed very little interest in pictures of scenery.

The photographer surveyed the tough hides of his audience, realizing he must overcome the obstacle of buyer resistance. "Pardon me, gentlemen. I see I have failed to explain the mesmerizing power of such a photograph. For upon a gaze—a single gaze," the photographer placed his hands over his heart, closed his eyes, and swooned, "Oh! Upon the gaze of a portrait of a real cowboy, the ladies are predisposed to fall all over in love with the bearer of such a photograph."

I don't think the boys knew exactly what the man was talking about, but if the ladies were ready to fall in love, they were all in. They lined up.

Looking through the lens, viewing the open-air baths, the photographer was just about to snap the picture. I glanced over and told Vern that he might be fronting a bit too much exposure for a first impression of introductory to a faint-hearted lady. Maybe he should holster himself down into the water.

Grinning and admiring our handsomeness, it was the first time we got to see a genuine likeness of ourselves. And, at a cost of four bits each, the photographer cleaned up.

The photographer appreciated my interest and offered me a fancy velvet-covered album with samples of his work to look at while he finished and packed up his wagon.

Some were scenes of the main streets of towns and farm houses with proud families sitting in buggies and chairs in the front yard. One picture was of a cow grazing on the roof of a sod house.

Then, I couldn't believe my eyes—

There was my Ginny in a flowered dress standing by an ore cart with a crew of miners. A second photograph presented her and a Negro woman standing under a shady tree with twelve men having a sit-down supper.

Turning the page revealed the most beautiful portrait of Ginny as I remembered her.

"Sure was a pretty one. A real heartbreaker," said the photographer looking over my shoulder.

"Where were these taken?" I asked.

"Oh, that was over in Black Canyon at the Silver Bell Mine." The photographer pointed to Maddy and went on. "Baked the best pies I ever ate. If you're ever around there, be sure—"

"How long ago?"

"Year . . . year and a half."

"Can I buy the portrait?"

"I'd rather not. It's one of my best samples."

I reached into my pocket, "I'll give you this twenty dollar gold piece for it."

15

"Let's Split Em"

Cowboying Wasn't All Glory—low wages, fleas and gray-backs, toothaches, tough water, and lonely nights so cold I'd wake up and run around to thaw out. A lot of these ride-along, jaw-breaking, brag-on weaners just aired their lungs and scattered cattle.

I lost track of time and Ginny. My eighteenth birthday and Christmas came and went. With just-paid wages, T-Bone, Adam and I raced, quirt and spur, to town with money to burn.

Ginny Paced Up And Down the wooden plank sidewalk in the little cattle town. The clock in the Arizona Stage Line station read: 7:52. The chalk-board read: "3:00 p.m. Stage is late." Weary travelers and their luggage were sprawled out waiting for the stage.

Ginny had made inquires in many towns and this main street was no different. She had spent the afternoon looking in windows and questioning store-keepers and townspeople if they had seen or were acquainted with a young man by the name of WB.

She told them he had been orphaned. She told them he had inherited a fortune . . . he was a war hero . . . a famous actor . . . her husband. She told them he was a cowboy. They appeared to respond to the drama and were more sympathetic and willing to try a little harder to recall him. Several recalled him vividly just to be helpful, but all were not.

She stopped and questioned two cowboys riding out of town. "He's my brother: 19, tall, thin, has four claw marks from a bear on his left arm, rides an Indian pony—answers to WB."

"Sorry. He don't sound at all familiar."

The other cowboy smiled and flirted, "You can take me home, sis. I'll be your brother."

Ginny laughed and they rode away. They turned and smiled eyeing the pretty sister.

Her stagecoach was late and she was debating whether or not to get a good meal and a night's rest before leaving in the morning.

The hotel clerk greeted her. "Hello, Ma'am. Any luck finding him?"

"No, thank you for asking."

The sound of barking dogs filled the street. She turned to see an arriving stagecoach. "I'll be checking out."

The stage came to a noisy, skidding stop and the lagging dust continued to move forward covering the stage and filling the passenger windows. "We're here! Right on time!" yelled the dusty driver gripping the reins. Before jumping down, he made an announcement: "They'll be a short whistle stop to change out the horses and for me to go over to the saloon and wet my whistle." He laughed at his own joke, "Thank you. See all passengers in thirty minutes."

Ginny crossed the street to take a last look in the saloon on the chance some cowboys had come in while she was down the street. She looked through the rippled-bubbled glass windows of the saloon as the stagecoach driver was greeted by piano music and a knowing barkeep. The barkeep poured him a shot—and another. . . .

The fresh horses were teamed up. The driver of the stagecoach held the door for Ginny. She was the last passenger to get into the coach. He gave her a hand. Stepping in, Ginny said, "You were not on time, sir. The stage was five hours late."

The well-greased surly driver matter-of-factly answered: "Well, there's town time and there's stage time. I travels on stage time." He closed the door.

The canvas mail-bag was handed up to the conductor in the driver's box. The driver climbed up and sat next to him taking hold of the reins. He had wet his whistle more than once and announced down to the passengers: "Watches and underwear ain't worth dying for, folks. If we gets held up, just hand 'em over." With that, he flapped the ribbons, "Get'a long! H'up, there!" and gave out a piercing whistle. Six horses lurched against their collars in union, traces snapped taut, metal fastenings clinked and the stage leaped into motion. The horses charged forward and the stagecoach bounded away down Main Street.

The three cowboys, T-Bone, Adam, and WB, raced up Main Street for their night on the town.

The driver elbowed the conductor and laughed: "Let's split 'em!" The cowboys reined quickly as the stagecoach rushed through them like a bowling ball approaching pins. They quickly split apart as the stagecoach roared through.

WB was the seven pin.

The town glowed like a beacon in the night and was a welcome distraction after three months on the trail. A loud and rowdy harbor with game, folly, and vice, served up to entertain and boost the spirits and wages of the lonesome and trail-weary.

We tied off our horses and with a jingle in our pockets, pushed through the swinging saloon doors into a haze of drifting smoke and wandered over the wooden floor, through a spirited corral of music, dancing, and laughter.

Drifters, cowboys, and gamblers were engaged in faro, dice, and roulette. The action was thick and fast.

In all its raucous gaiety, the reckless hands— touchy as scorpions, were trailin' for trouble—it was 'bout too noisy to bear.

Bellied up to the bar with one foot on the brass rail, we stood in awe staring at the huge oversized painting of a reclining woman, robust in form, revealed in all her splendor.

Blushing, an aberration of delight widened our eyes, when all of a sudden she appeared to breathe and quiver.

The barkeep interrupted our vision, "Ain't she a beauty? . . . What can I get you, boys?—whiskey, mule punch, bloody gut, mescal?" Grinning at our distraction, waiting for our answer, he asked, "Haven't you boys never seen a naked lady before?"

"No!" we answered.

Leaning in with eyes wide open, "See that!" gestured Adam. "She's breathing again!"

Smiling and without looking at the painting, the barkeep just laughed, "You boys are dreamin', been out on the trail too long—"

"Look! Look!" I pointed, "She's doing it again."

Laughing, the barkeep poured us a whiskey, "This one's on the house, boys." And then I noticed the reflection in a mirror from behind the bar. The barkeep's foot, slow and steady, was squeezing air from a bellows connected to a rubber tube snaked up behind the 'breathtaking' painting, which explained her lively performance.

Bamboozled, we laughed. This was our night to howl—and howl we did! . . .

Full of folly, we crawled onto our horses and flashed our Colts, blazing from the jamboree whoopin'.

Adam had gotten into a rough-and-tumble over something—cards, whiskey, night-blooming flowers—and returned to camp with a fogged eye. From then on, we called him Punch.

T-Bone roostered, slickered, and in need of money

to cover his losses with Lady Luck, sold me his batwing chaps with the silver *conchos*. He wore 'em to town and I wore 'em back. Real beauties.

Stumbling into the bunkhouse, Punch helped me get T-Bone inside. A lantern spilled its light over a game of cards. The boys weren't smiling and lingered about in their long johns. Cowboys didn't stay around long after the last drive to market.

Raking in the pot, Shakes, one of the wranglers, greeted us, "Welcome back, girls. Been waitin' on ya." The rest of the hands climbed out of their bed rolls. "The old man stopped by, says he's going to miss us." Shuffling the cards, Shakes announced, "Time to cut the cards, boys." Slapping the cards on the table, he knocked the deck, "Jacks or better—ride out."

Glum hands, we cut the cards. Mine was the queen of hearts. "See you in the spring, boys."

I took a day. Parting company with the outfit was hard. Parting company with Arrow was even harder, but it was time. He was ready for pension. The old man said he'd keep an eye on him. I turned him out to pasture in good feed.

"We had a good run, partner. You carried me faithfully in good humor all the way across country and to the mines and back."

Arrow put his muzzle against my chest and we just stood there . . . it was more than an emotional moment. I was barely able to get the words out of my mouth.

"It's time for you to slow down . . . take 'r easy. Arrow, you're in good hands." With sadness in my heart I turned to walk away. Arrow slowly started to follow. "Not today, partner." I kept walking.

I shod my new rangy sorrel, cleaned my saddle blanket, tied a half hitch with a keeper with the cantle strings around my slicker and was on my way.

Getting an early start before sunup, I was riding out when I saw the old man squatting by the coffee fire poking the coals. What's he doing up so early? I moseyed over to say my good bye. The old man's face was seamed by sun and toil. He was focused on the flames of the fire.

Without looking up, he poured coffee into a tin cup and handed it to me as I got off my horse. Not lifting his eyes, he just kept stirring the coals. "Good coffee, sir." I said. No response. He's fixed on the altar of the fire. Well, standing around with distant, company I finished my coffee. "I'll be on my way." I bent down to set my cup on the fire pit rock, "Thank you, sir. I sure appreciate all you've done for me . . . and for keeping an eye on Arrow."

Still not turning to face me, he said, "You did real good, cowboy." As I stood up, so did he. With wet eyes he gave me a hug, "You did real good, son."

It was an emotional moment that had us both drying an eye. . . . Enough said. I swung aboard and he went back to poking the fire.

As I rode away, I heard the old man's final words. "Next time you see Sunny, give him my heartfelt hello."

"Yes, sir, I surely will."

I closed the gate on my way out.

16

A LONESOME GO

LEAVING THE OLD MAN was the second hardest thing I'd ever had to do.

It was a lonesome go. I made my rounds to other towns—Mesa, Prescott, Florence—posting my letters for the Harts and Ginny during the off-seasons.

On my way to Yuma, while riding out along the cliffs, I came across a painter-artist of pictures engaged in his painting. I sat quietly watching him from my horse. He captured the feeling of the wild mustangs flying across the range and I pictured myself riding them.

The artist finished a detail with a flourish and said, "Hello."

"Howdy. You're real good with those saguaros, puffy clouds, and mountains."

"Thank you."

"How long ago did those mustangs pass by?"

The artist laughed, "They're long gone, cowboy."

Before he traveled on, he sold me a small box of colors and brushes and showed me a thing or two about perspective and contrast. I learned how to mix primary colors and paint with tint, tone, and shade.

During the in-betweens, I'd go off and paint a picture, trying to copy the afternoon light on the peaks and the billowing clouds floating over the range. The artist told me he was trying to capture the drama of the stormy western skies. I tried to capture the freedom of the wild mustangs galloping across the range.

THE STAGECOACH WAS A DUSTY SPECK, bounding across the vast Arizona desert blazing with color.

It was a rough ride inside the coach. Ginny laughed out loud repeatedly. "Sorry." She looked around sheepishly eying the other passengers. She was consumed by the book she was reading and laughed to herself as she turned the page.

"Do you find the book amusing, Ginny?" asked the sharply dressed, handsome red-haired young man from back East sitting across from her.

Ginny looked up over the top of the book and sat it down in her lap. "Most exuberant, Mr. Clemens, extremely amusing, full of truths and fanciful half-truths. I rather doubt miners raked in a thousand dollars worth of gold out of their claims in a day. Most were lucky if they were able to buy a pie at the end of the day. But as the author wrote in the book, 'If they did have a good day, they were broke in the morning.' "

"Everyone's a critic," smiled the man. "Do you think the author has a future in the craft?"

"Are you at all familiar with the author, sir?"

"Yes, I am. Fairly well, as a mater-of-fact."

"Oh, well then, most assuredly, sir! He has a vivid imagination and a flare for the humorous that allow us to laugh at ourselves. Although at times he is rather irreverent. Do you agree?"

BY THE WARM GLOW of a campfire, I felt closest to Ginny while composing letters to her: "Ginny, my love . . . My dearest Ginny . . . Ginny, darling, all I possess are cherished memories of you, my love, that linger in my marrow. . . ." I penned letters of love expressing the joy and fantasies of my heart, and then closed with, "I shall carry on my roam until we are together again. I belong to you."

I was riding on a remote road between nowhere and lost, when a stagecoach approached me from behind. I stood in the middle of the road and waved it down. The first words out of the driver's mouth were: "Do you know where you are, cowboy?"

"No, sir, thought I was on the road to Yuma."

The driver swung his arm around in a wide arc pointing back to where he had just come from. "You missed the cut-off 'bout a mile back."

"Thank you, sir. What's your destination?"

The conductor spoke up: "We're on a roundy-round. A lot of places, all the way to Santa Fe in New Mexico Territory, and back round again."

I handed my bundle of sonnets over to the conductor. "I'd like you to post these letters to wherever you're headed. One to every post office you pass along the way."

The conductor counted and looked over the

letters . . . "General delivery. Miss—" He hefted the bundle, and grinned, "Well, if your letters don't find her, there sure are some pretty gals in Tucson."

I paid the postage and thanked them. "Here's a little something for your trouble." I watched the stagecoach roll away and turned back headed for the Yuma cut-off.

Inside the coach, the leather window curtains were rolled down for shade and to keep out the dust. Ginny was asleep with her book, *Roughing It* sitting on her lap. Opened to the inside cover page, it was personally autographed:

> *"Ginny, A fine appraisal.*
> *Truly Yours, Mark Twain"*

In Yuma, I posted a letter and inquired of the postmaster about the Harts. The postmaster accepted my letter but had no recollection of the Harts. A flurry of gunshots from outside interrupted our conversation and I left.

Down the street, a cowboy was spinning around on his horse, dusting up the road, firing lead plums into the air from his six-shooter, attracting attention. "Cowboys! Cowboys! Wranglers! The Rocking ⨼ is hiring on hands," shouted the cowboy.

The cowboy's name was Shorty and I hired on.

Riding for the ⨼ I had my own *remuda*—a string of seven or nine horses.

When you chose a horse, you partnered up. Cattle would charge a walking man. I never did anything alone.

My life depended on whichever horse I was riding.

17

Nighthawking

I WAS NIGHTHAWKING riding Quincy. Gentle, sure-footed, and with a good sense of direction, he kept one eye on the cattle and one eye on the trail. And, he could tell time—he'd stop, shake his head, and drift back to camp knowing our two-hour watch was over, whether I was awake or not, and circle the chuck wagon until I smelled the coffee.

We had gathered and were sitting on a ⌣ herd, mostly yearlings, tallied just short of fifteen hundred head. The weather was hot, night and day, threatening to storm. The moon was on the rise and the cattle chewed their cuds, grunting and blowing over contented stomachs. I enjoyed the night motion of the moon and stars. I had just passed my nineteenth birthday. Watching the Dipper swing around the North Star, I imagined Ginny looking into the glimmering heavens, gazing on our Moon. I longed for my prairie rose. Her love warmed me.

My harmonica playing was improving. It didn't scare the cattle any more. I was playing a lullaby I learned from Aiden. Nervous as cats, my playing had a way of settling 'em down for the night.

The hands were touchy over the strain of the drive, but no one was complaining. I had just gotten to sleep when Jorge, one of the guards nighthawking with us, rousted me out by bouncing pebbles off my head. Startled awake I jerked, quick-fingered, reaching for my six-shooter. It was just before daybreak. Coyotes were howling. It was my second trick at watch with him and Carver. Carver was a Negro cowboy, afraid of owls, but he nearly had their vision at night.

It was a foggy morning. I rode up slowly to relieve grizzly Bump, one of the night guards making rounds on the herd. I found him asleep in the saddle. Bump never said much. As a matter of fact, the only time he opened his mouth was to feed it.

Riding alongside Bump, tipping and tilting in his saddle, we circled the herd twice, passing Carver and Jorge who were circling and eyeing the herd in the opposite direction. They just smiled. I tapped Bump with my quirt. Groggy, he opened his eyes, and without a word reined off back to camp.

Circling the herd, humming a tune, milling my thoughts, I became aware I was holding Ginny's pearl button in my hand, polishing it with my thumb. It glistened in the moonlight. Tallying off the years on my fingers: 1874, '75, '76, it had been three years and I could still feel her heart beat.

I had sent letters addressed general delivery, Mr. and Mrs. Virgil Hart, attention: Ginny, to every town, whistle stop, and military outpost, in the West.

Dozing off, barely awake, my thoughts were of Ginny. Real in my dreams, the melody of her voice played a tune in my heart. She was woven into the fabric of my imagination. Memories of Ginny flooded my head. They were all I had left. As one image drifted away, another washed in: Ginny's soft kiss and caress of the scar on my arm . . . her laughter at me playing a tinny tune . . . our reflection in the ripples and rings of the brook.

Asleep in the saddle, I sang out, "Swing them pretty girls round and round." I dreamed of her dancing at the schoolhouse baile—twirling and swirling, spinning and dipping. "Ginny," I asked, "May I have this dance?"

"Oh, I'm sorry, sir, my dance card is filled." And she whirled away.

And then it occurred to me, "Oh no!" I burst out. What if she has wed a finer life, forgotten me, and now plays with a parcel-load of young ones? I was startled awake.

Carver was riding alongside listening to my sleep talk. He grinned, "I'll bet your Ginny's a real peach."

"Yes, she truly is."

We circled the herd when the morning air charged up. Our horses shivered and we felt the breeze.

A storm was brewing.

18

THE EARTH QUIVERED

THUNDER, LIGHTNING, AND WIND — the earth quivered. "Smell that? . . . Here she comes!" announced Carver. Echoing his pronouncement, the cries of honking wild geese anticipating the rage of the storm were fleeing overhead.

"We're gonna get wet." We pulled our hats down hard with both hands.

Black-purple storm clouds rolled in over the mountain range with the full force of Moses determined to flood hell. We tried to hold the stirring cattle on the bed ground. Quicker than a cat can blink, drops of rain the size of cherries pounded on my hat. Lightning struck the distant horizon setting the desert sage grass ablaze.

"1 — 2 — 3," counted Carver . . . and with a mighty clap, thunder shook Heaven and Earth reverberating and rumbling across the range.

Flash fires roared, racing over the parched mesa. The faint sound of the chuck's triangle rang out and every boot in camp was in the saddle.

Caught under the thick blanket of black rolling storm clouds, the desert darkened. The rains poured down out of the sky with such force, the raging fires that had engulfed Skull Mesa were extinguished like breath on a candle.

The Sun, Moon, and Stars disappeared. The sky turned blacker than the inside of a mine. Driving rain pelted down with the cutting force of a gale turning the dry, hard desert into slippery mud.

Thunder clapped and the herd was up-off, on the run with a roaring rush, charging Carver and me. We had no choice but to whirl and lead the stampede.

"We're riding into hell!" I yelled.

"No! We're already there!" howled Carver.

Jamming the wind we rode blind, leading the charging frenzy. Full-out we raced for our lives. One stumble and the raging herd would be pounding over us.

In the sound and fury—flying blind in the dark—I could only see the cattle in the flickers of lightning zigzagging through the crackling clouds.

The gale winds howled—the thunder rolled— and the rumble turned into one deafening drone.

Frantic, the seething wild mass of vast reserve blasted with smashing hooves and clacking horns towards the high-cut banks of the creek. I couldn't see my horse's head, so I gave him the reins, praying he could negotiate the perils of the rough terrain.

With a blinding flash and crash of thunder, a bolt of lightening struck the herd. The electric discharge spooled and curled, flashing around their horns, sizzling and snapping, leaping from steer to steer. The herd was aglow. Their fierce, frightened eyes dazzled, sparkling like emeralds.

Terrified, the roaring herd moved as a massive wave in a howling sea—rising and falling—raging across the desert.

Slipping and sliding, it was all we could do to stick to our saddles. We raced the lighting and thundering hooves, trying to swing the leaders and mill the herd into a round-and-round. Blind, in the mucky thick of it, running pell-mell for miles, we raced death. One misstep and we'd be done in.

The thunderclap 'bout made my ears bleed and the lightning saved my life. Lightning flashed and right before my eyes, I watched Carver, now air-borne, arms flailing, with his horse falling out from under him. The raging cattle were tumbling over the edge and falling from the high bluffs, plunging down into the creek.

My horse dug his forefeet into the muddy earth. With his hind feet well under him, he stopped short of the edge with such force, my face slammed into his head. Bloody and dazed, I grabbed a fistful of mane and held on for life.

In the flashes of lightning, I saw Indians from their caves in the caliche cliffs watching the river of cattle piling up in the creek. The thunder rolled and torrents of rain sluiced down washing over the bawling stacks, of steaming cattle.

We had stayed with the herd and now there was

nothing I could do. I sat in the thundering darkness, as if in church. *Dios sabe*, why wasn't I at the bottom of the pile-up? Feeling my horse's heart beating like a drum, I sat there perched on the edge dazed and blurry-eyed, bleeding and trembling, drenched in the throbbing rain. . . .

I hadn't noticed the rain had stopped until I felt the warmth and glory of the morning rays of sunlight on my face. The cattle were still. Standing stiff in place facing the creek, they sniffed the sweet breath of dawn crowned in the luminous light of a morning rainbow.

I called out, shattering the peaceful sounds of morning. "Carver! . . . Carver!" There was no answer. My face clouded in the shadows of death. I took off my hat and said a silent prayer . . . "And may his spirit return to the Giver."

19

BLUE WHISTLERS

THE WASHES RAGED, flowing with rolling muddy water, violently carrying full-grown mesquite trees away and out of sight. Huge boulders tumbled like marbles, rolling past floating cattle and horses, taking out cottonwoods as if they were tinker pins in a child's game.

Sacked in their saddles, we lost two good men. Grim and silent, we buried them by the hackberry trees up in the foothills overlooking the open range. It was a grey day threatening to rain, when the funeral cortege rode up the hill leading the two horses carrying their bodies to the gravesite. The wind whistled and the rain began to drizzle.

Covered in their slickers and wrapped gently in their saddle blankets, we laid them low into their wet bunks already filling with water. We shoveled in the dirt, tamped it smooth and overlaid rocks.

A plank shelf from the chuck wagon had been cut and two headboards carved to mark the graves. Ernestro, the outfit's cook, had a flair with the blade and carved the letters real fancy:

Jorge Vásquez
Californio Vaquero
1876

I didn't know Jorge that well, but I liked him and his nature. Carver was a Sergeant in the 9th Cavalry, an all-Negro regiment, formed by the United States after the Rebellion. Dependable, self-contained—as good a horseman as I've ever shared a trail with.

On Carver's headboard, Ernestro cut:

Carver Butler
Buffalo Soldier
1876

We hung his brass bugle on the headboard.

Being all the family they had, the outfit removed their hats and silently readied for a cowboy's prayer over them. Fogged with our own feelings and grief, we all waited for someone to say the prayer.

With two black eyes from slamming into my horse's head, I stood there thinking, I'll not be taking tomorrow for granted.

Words did not easily rise to the occasion. Our spurs rattled lowly.

"They were my best friends! Brothers!" blurted Shorty. "Now they're with God—"

"Amen!" retorted the outfit.

We fired salutes of blue whistlers from our six-shooters into the sky, mounted up, and silently trailed back to camp. Ernestro walked, carrying the shovel.

There was work to be done.

GINNY, IN A FLORAL DRESS, sat alone in an empty church. The noonday church bell began to toll.

Virgil listened to the tolling bell, watching the church from his window in the coach as the stage arrived in the bustling western town.

He had been making the rounds of other towns in search of Ginny. The stagecoach slowed to a stop. The conductor announced, "We made it! This is it! We're here!"

Virgil climbed down from the coach and grabbed his grip. The church bell was still tolling, he smiled. He would say a prayer for Ginny at the church—but, right now he was hungry. He looked up and down the town's wooden storefronts, busy with wagons, cowboys and townspeople. A restaurant was right across the street and it was crowded—a good sign that they served decent food.

Light streamed in on Ginny through the side windows of the church. She looked like an angel transfixed in soft prayer. "If WB is alive, may I find him and if I do not, keep him safe." After a long while Ginny got up, placed an offering in the donation box and left.

Walking to town, Ginny thought about her parents. It had been three years since she had left them. A sign in the window of a restaurant caught her eye: *Fresh Baked Pies*. She smiled and thought of Maddy. She decided to get a piece of fruit pie.

Virgil was seated and eating with his back to the door. He and the rest of the customers were annoyed by the loud, rowdy behavior of four range hands seated at a table across the room.

The restaurant door opened to the sound of a bell fixed to a spring on the door. Ginny entered and looked around for a seat. She did not see Virgil, she saw Eddy, the rude, coarse skinny-dipping range-rat. "Well, look at ya'll shined up real purdy like a catalogue picture," shouted Eddy.

Eddy stood up and gestured, "Oh, by all means, mad-moiselle, join us please."

"Please mad-mozell," echoed Barlow. The other two mules at the table laughed along. Ginny turned to leave, when Eddy sniped: "WB wuz in our outfit all along, Ginny. I hope I didn't cause yew any inconvenience."

Virgil turned when he heard WB's name—and saw Ginny—his girl had grown up.

Virgil contained himself, anxiously watching the confrontation.

"Whoa! This is sweet tart!" sniped Barlow.

A silent hush came over the restaurant. Ginny's face flushed red.

"Bet yur so mad you could spit. Huh," sneered Eddy.

Ginny slowly walked across the restaurant to their table, paused then slapped Eddy full-handed.

Eddy took the slap and returned one right back—

Virgil was up, moving between the tables with the speed of anger and the rumble of thunder.

The herd of range-rats surrounded him.

Barlow swung, Virgil dodged. This fight was over. The rats didn't know it yet. Virgil was a hammer looking for nails. Left - right - left - three fast jabs - three faces were bleeding.

Barlow tried again. Virgil countered with a solid punch that spun Barlow flailing into the arms of Eddy. A fist came from behind and slid off Virgil's ear. He grabbed the arm connected to it and twisted it around - snapping it behind his back. He wanted these bullies to feel pain. Virgil moved with precision and punched with power.

There was a lot of cracking and snapping. He bloodied their faces and broke their bones so they would have plenty of time to think about their low character while they recuperated.

One of the mules pulled his six-shooter. Virgil grabbed it - spun it - and hammered a smashing blow to the gunfighter's forehead with the butt of the gun. Virgil blocked a boot kicking with a snapping twist, flipping the man over the table. He served up a heaping helping of bone and knuckle.

Eddy jumped him from behind. Virgil heaved him over his head and stood Eddy up in front of him. Shaky Eddy looked around. He was the last rat standing. Virgil made an edgy move. Eddy jerked back. Virgil leaned in towards Eddy and said, "Bet yur so mad you could spit. Huh." Eddy was a fright. "I'm that purdy catalog picture's father."

Eddy didn't see the hammer coming.

127

20

GLOOMY COMPANY

THE STORM was like grandma's mixing bowl.
Rocks, cactus, trees, and limbs all whipped up every
which way, frosted with mud, berries, cactus pads,
and sage grass, then finely decorated with the
embossed tracks of quail, deer, javelina, and coyote.

Turkey buzzards made lazy circles in the sky.

The cattle were scattered and many were lost.
I'm sure the Indians made good use of them.

We all squished in our boots for days and
prowled for weeks rounding up horses and scouring
for cattle as far as ten miles away.

I lost Ginny's pearl button in the fury of the
stampede—mixed up somewhere in the sea of mud.

The storm had come and gone but the clouds of discontent lingered. Memories of Jorge and Carver played heavy on our minds.

The mood of the outfit turned gloomy. Summer work was long over. With little work to keep us busy, our minds started to drift with thoughts of winter coming on.

Seven of us, what was left of the outfit, were out on the range circled up sitting on our horses, pondering our future.

"It's all I can do to put up with all your sour company," drawled Shorty, trying to lighten our mood.

"Ya won't hav' t' much longer," quipped Lyle.

"Brandin's just about wrapped up—waddies are all gone. We're next," said Cardy.

Bump sat silently listening to our wallow.

G Jakes looked around, surrounded by sad sacks. "Christmas comin' on—I got nowhere to go. Where ya all thinkin' 'bout holin' up to spring?"

"Tank and I was thinkin' about trying on Mexico," answered Punch.

"*Señoritas! Olé!*" sang Shorty, all smiles.

"I'll ride down to Mexico with you, Punch," I said, looking at the distant faces. Like me, most of the boys were rootless and strays. We didn't have families with hearth fires and warm hearts to embrace us.

The days stayed wet and the nights turned cold.

Ernestro, a mushroom of a man, managed his chuck peeking out from the shade of a large sombrero. A couple of the hands, in muddy boots, raised his cook fire with rocks until the ground dried out. Ernestro shoveled gravel to fill the spaces between the rocks. Firewood for cooking was scarce.

The only bright cloud was seeing El Book ride into camp. I greeted him. "El Book, *amigo. Hace tan tiempo.*"

El Book smiled. "*Hola mi amigo.* You remember pretty good."

"Where are you headed?"

"California, to visit my family for Christmas. Perhaps I can spend the night? A hot meal?"

"Perhaps you have a good story."

Smiling, "Perhaps—"

Something whizzed by our heads—and another. We ducked.

Our impassioned cook was flinging buffalo chips at the cowhands. He spoke in roaring Spanish when he was upset, "*Cocino no más sobre buffalo chippy!*"

El Book laughed. "No more cooking over buffalo chips!"

The cowboys dodged and quickly jumped out of the way of the flying chips.

Ernestro had run out of patience. "There will be cold beans!—cold coffee!—cold everything!—if you waddies don't gather up some wood—good dry wood for Ernestro's fire."

I introduced El Book to Ernestro. They hit it off and in a few words of Spanish they were engaged in preparing a meal. Glad the outfit had a *cocinero*—cook—El Book enjoyed Ernestro's spicy cooking and decided to stay on for awhile.

What Ernestro didn't know about peppers, El Book did—compadres of the flame.

I hooked a loop around the root of a large dead cholla cactus and yanked it out of the wash.

My horse gave a snort and lunged to one side. Disturbed, a rattlesnake uncoiled from beneath the cactus, striking out. My horse reared. I drew my six-shooter, shot and holstered. As quick as that, the snake flopped dead at my horse's hooves.

I dragged the tree back to camp. About to break off the branches for firewood, I noticed bits of tied-off canvas and tattered colored cloth. And then it struck me. This is it!—the thorny, spiked sentry of the trail I had slammed into years ago, the painful day I was abruptly separated from Ginny. Looking over the broken tree, I had an idea.

I dug a hole between the chuck wagon and the campfire, stood the tree up and buried what was left of the gnarled root.

Ernestro, a jolly sight alright wearing an XXXX flour sack for an apron, enjoyed pointing out WB's tree for the outfit's amusement. They laughed accusing me of trying to grow firewood. Every day upon my return to camp for meals, he religiously watered that dead cholla tree with cold coffee, teasing in broken English, "Ernestro's coffee makes WB's tree grow big and strong."

Well, the tree just stood there until Ernestro went around on the sly, gathering up green leaves and stuck them on the dead limbs. Later that night he acted surprised announcing to the outfit, "Leaves! The tree is growing leaves!"

I took a lot of ribbing around that campfire. One after another, puffin' wind, the hands were relentless. "Yes, sir, we'll be eatin' peaches from WB's orchard in the morning."

The spirit of our outfit started to grow.

21

IT STARTED TO GROW

AN OLD MEXICAN SPUR with silver inlay and a large rowel appeared on one of the tree limbs. A day later, a little amber glass medicine bottle hung from a branch wired up with a length of bailing-wire.

The next night, while spilling stories around the campfire, we noticed a boot stuck on the end of a branch. The flickering shadows from the fire made it appear that the boot was dancing.

No one ever saw who was dressing up the tree, but it was definitely growing. From one boot, it now had four—enough for a square dance. The tree also wore a faded blue neckerchief and some horseshoes. A red jasper stone, polished by the creek, balanced between the trunk and a limb. The tree now had a heart.

And still, during all that time, none of the hands ever owned up to fooling with the tree, even though two of the old boots looked like Shorty's.

Every time I crossed paths with the tree, there was another eye-catcher onboard. A hand-woven black and white horse-hair lariat was looped up and down and around the branches circling the tree. Colorful river stones, white quartz, turquoise, and dangling shards of hand-decorated Indian pottery adorned the branches. Fanciful attractions of brass rosettes, cobbled together with sticks, strings, and feathers, now twisted in the wind.

As the tree grew, so did our spirits and the laughter around the campfire. We accused each other of sneaking around, dressing up the tree. "Where did that huge pinecone come from?" asked Lyle. We were all pretty sure it came from Lyle.

In a matter of a few days I was afraid the tree's branches would collapse under their own weight. Canning jars, peach cans with holes punched in them, and shiny tin lids flashed in the sunlight.

Ernestro riled early one morning when he discovered the *ristra*, his string of red Mexican peppers, was missing from the chuck, taken apart and now hanging like fruit all over the tree. At breakfast he surveyed our faces, looking for the culprit or culprits who likely fooled with his peppers. Grinning and eyeing each other, the outfit stifled laughter.

Later that afternoon, Bump made up for our transgression of the peppers when he presented a delighted Ernestro with his cowboy hat filled with hen fruit—speckled wild turkey eggs, for Christmas breakfast.

22

OUT OF THE DARKNESS

CHRISTMAS EVE WAS UPON US. The Moon hung bright in the western sky, placed there by the hand of God, as an ornament in the fields of twinkling stars decorating the earth.

The horses and kitchen mules shivered and shook in the crisp desert night air, extending their heads over the makeshift corral to watch the commotion.

We gathered around our Christmas tree sharing cheer, good will, and the warmth of the fire. I cut a candle into pieces and placed them into the canning jars and peach cans. They glowed real pretty.

There was cowboy boasting with old tales that may have once had a speck of truth to them, but through years of retelling had soared with imagination to full-out fancy.

Lyle's laughing, he's crying, braggin' on glory days. "So Tank and me's trailin' beef, a mixed herd of Spanish Longhorns, from the Brazos country in Texas. Tank takes first night guard and falls sound asleep. It's quiet as a graveyard. No one bothers to wake 'em. His hoss goes to roundin' up strays.

Well, all night long his hoss does the work fo' both of 'em, headin' off and retrievin' cows. Come mornin' when the rest of the hands ride up ready to head out, here's Tank circlin'—still asleep. But now there are about twenty, thirty buffalo bedded down, enjoyin' the good company of the herd—"

"Now there you go again stretching the wire, Lyle. There was only nine or ten of them buffaloes," protested Tank.

Lyle shrugged, "So then, them Texas boys wanted to know where we 'learned cow' and if mama had any more boys at home like us."

"I bet they did," grinned Punch. "That's some windy tale, Lyle. You're startin' to collect flies—"

"That's the Texas truth!" roared Lyle.

"That's when cows climb trees," popped Cardy.

Shined boots and buckles, clean shirts and smiles, we toasted and clinked our cups. Merriment all around until the mules brayed, the horses riled, and the trail dog barked, sensing a presence off in the darkness.

Tank reached for a rifle, and shouted, "Who's out there?" Cocking his Winchester, "Show yourselves!"

A stranger's voice answered out, "Hold on. I'm alone. I'm coming in." Riding slowly out of the darkness of the cold desert night into our firelight, a stranger on a steaming horse appeared. To our surprise, he was followed by three snorting, steaming wild mustangs.

Wearing a serape, he was a striking cowboy with a mustache over a smile and chin beard. He had an easy way. Reining up and dismounting his lathered horse, he said, "These mustangs wear no brand. Found 'em on the range. Figured they might be yours."

Tank replied, "No, they ain't ours, stranger," disengaging the hammer and lowering his rifle.

With a gesture of his hand, the stranger said, "Then, consider 'em my gift. I'm traveling light tonight."

Well, we were all pretty amazed. I never saw wild mustangs follow anything but the sun and their own shadows. And I'm sure neither did El Book or any of the wranglers.

Looking around, the stranger said, "It's been a long ride. And the wind blows cold. Be alright with you fellas if I share your fire?"

Tank nodded, observing the horses. "Join us. You've been traveling fast. Racin' the devil are ya?"

The stranger began to strip the gear off his horse and grinned, "I'm working on it." The three wild mustangs stood by pawing dirt.

"Where y'all goin' in such a hurry?" Tank inquired. "These hosses are spent—"

"Feed and water's over here, partner," interrupted Bump, speaking up, amazing us all.

"Well now, ain't Bump overflowing with words," quipped Punch.

"Much obliged." The stranger motioned, "Git." His horse moved off with Bump and the three mustangs followed along. Turning back to Tank, he answered, "I'm riding to town to celebrate my birth."

Ernestro walked up grinning hospitality and handed the stranger a cup of cheer. "Happy Birthday, *amigo*. And, *Feliz Navidad*. This'll warm you up."

The stranger smiled with appreciation, *"Feliz Navidad."* He looked at me and the rest of the outfit, "Thank you all for your fire."

Celebrating the spirit of Christmas, the stranger joined our circle of stories, tales, and show. G Jakes, good with rope tricks, skipped in and out of a loop twirling it from side to side, showing off his stuff.

The stranger listened and laughed as El Book spun a funny story about a coyote, mule, and the frog.

Ernestro poured wine from a jug into 'cowboy crystal'—canning jars he had saved for the occasion. Shorty passed the jars around. Ernestro raised his jar and proposed a toast, *"Feliz Navidad."* Raising our jars, we returned the toast, *"Feliz Navidad."*

It was Ernestro's night to shine and he was ready. Missing a finger, he had a reputation for his one-finger chili. Tonight we would feast on his chili verde and corn tamales, both holiday favorites. A wagon plank was rigged to the chuck wagon and set up with bowls and baskets of mesquite-smoked corn bread.

Bump was winning at a fast game of checkers. Punch pondered, planning his next move. "King me."

It was a dandy party, jolly all around sharing the holiday spirit.

Ernestro removed the Dutch ovens from the coals. Striking the chuck's triangle, he announced, "Chili time!"

As the night unfolded, the stranger trailed into a story, a word, something to say to each one of us.

Laughing with enthusiasm, he told his own bronc-busting story. "Screwed on tight, I was ready. The roan left the ground pawin' at the moon. He was flyin' so crooked, all I could see were the birds in the sky. He was so high, you could see mountain peaks and tree tops 'neath him. Then we parted company. He sailed me through the air and I fell from the clouds, bustin' the earth."

I was gazing at the moon when the stranger wandered over and saw the harmonica in my pocket. "You any good with that harp?"

"The cattle like it."

He smiled, "May I?" I handed it over. Tapping it on his hand, he paused, "You know, riding in tonight, I spotted a number of mustangs and wild cattle up in the hills along the ridges, bushed up, hidden in the mesquites and roughs. Good pickin's for a brush popper."

"A storm came through awhile ago and really scattered 'em." Studying the stranger, he struck me familiar and I asked, "Have we met before?"

"Maybe so. I've been a lot of places. Ever been to Santa Fe?"

"No, sir. Is that where you got your hat?"

The stranger smiled proudly, shaping the broad brim. "Nice one, isn't it?"

"It fits you fine," I said. "Best I've seen.

Mouthing the harmonica, he said, "This is a favorite of mine." He began to play.

"I never heard that one. What's it called?"

"The Cowboy's Lament."

"I like it."

Draining the last of the wine into a jar, Ernestro

slammed down the empty wine jug and loudly announced, "We's outta wine!"

We laughed, "Outta wine? What? You just don't know how to pour a jug." The stranger glanced over at the jug, laughing, enjoying the moment.

Ernestro snapped back in good humor, "I know how to work a jug." He jerked it up over his head to show the jug was empty. Wine gushed out, splashing him. We all roared with laughter. The merriment around the fire and our Christmas tree continued as we enjoyed our meal and each other's company.

Boomer, best catch dog I ever saw, jumped in and out of a spinning loop for treats. Bits and pieces of cowboy yarns and tales peppered the night: "Remember Pack Rat's raucous, runaway mules breakin' free from the wagon? They's draggin' their rings 'n trace chains, rattlin' 'n skiddin' over them flint rocks—sparkin' 'n blazin' up trails of fire!"

Over by the fire, the stranger put the cover back on the Dutch oven. He and Ernestro were engaged in a spirited conversation in Spanish, with animated gestures of chopping, stirring, and rolling like two cooks sharing recipes and secrets. The stranger must have liked the chili verde. Ernestro put two canning jars of it in his saddlebags and cheerfully wrapped up some of the mesquite-smoked cornbread as well.

The spirit and bonds of fellowship shined as the candles on the tree glowed. I pulled out my harmonica and began playing the only Christmas hymn I knew, *"Silent Night."*

One by one, the cowboys removed their hats. Standing around our Christmas tree, the warm glow on their faces as I played, was a sight for poor eyes.

23

THANKS FOR YOUR SONG

EARLY CHRISTMAS MORNING, awakened by the lingering smell of smoke and coffee on the coals, we heard Ernestro's jolly voice, "Shine and arise, waddies. *Feliz Navidad.* Give glory to God."

We slowly wandered up to the breakfast fire. Ernestro was cracking turkey eggs into a skillet when he glanced up at the Christmas tree. *"Gloria a Dios!"* he whispered to himself. Rising up and not believing his eyes, he stumbled backwards.

The golden rays of the morning sun highlighted the now much-alive cholla, abloom with red blossoms and yellow fruit hanging from the barbed, ocher branches. Cactus wrens chirped and flittered about the blossoms.

In awe and wonder, we slowly approached our Christmas tree. Struck by a ray of sunlight, the stranger's cowboy hat hung on a branch. I carefully removed it from the tree. Inside the hat was a note. I read it aloud to the camp:

"WB,
Thank you for your song.
You'll find Ginny in Santa Fe.
Merry Christmas. God bless you all.
– Sunny"

Well, we all stood there looking in amazement at the tree and each other.

I put on the cowboy hat. It was a good fit.

Asking around about the trail to Santa Fe, El Book had more than the answer. "Fly to your darling *querida.*" And with a flair for romance, he told me, "You will want to ride the old Spanish trail from California that crosses the Arizona Territory to New Mexico, and then to the town of romance, *La Villa Real de la Santa Fe de San Francisco de Assisi.*" It rolled off his tongue like a song. And with a big smile added, "Called 'Santa Fe' by the Americano." He went on to say, "*La Villa* was built in 1611 when Spain owned all the known land to the north and west of the Mississippi River to the Pacific Ocean."

24

READY, BUTTON?

NEW MEXICO figured to be a long ride. I picked up my lariat and saddle. Looking over the horses in the camp's corral, the mustangs Sunny gifted the outfit took my eye. Three year olds, they were probably just shedding the last of their colt teeth. I especially liked the grulla mustang, grey with shades of purple. He was big for a mustang. My guess was he's almost sixteen hands.

The cowboys made their way to the rail. Topping off a bronc always made for a good show. Thinking this ought to be fun, they weren't betting on WB.

We cut the other horses from the corral. Having busted my share of rough strings, this mustang appeared to be more horse than any bronc I'd ever broke. I built a fast loop as I entered the corral. The mustang circled around, sizing me up, out of the corner of his eye. He's probably thinking, 'This won't take long, button.'

I tried to look fearless while thinking about taking an ear, getting him down, and tying foot-ropes. With him down, I could lace up my saddle, slide on, and ride him up.

The hands were all worked up, looking for a good time.

Sparring with me, the mustang stopped. Working his ears, he swung his head, and circled me in the opposite direction, challenging my courage. Cocking the rope, I let the loop fly. The rope hissed, singing as it left my hand. I was ready to dally the rope around the snubbing post. But the loop flopped and the boys went wild.

Reloading, I gathered up the rope and shook out a quick loop. The mustang snorted, reversed his direction, and raced around the corral. But before I could throw again, he cut up the center, and abruptly hit a dead stop.

I got the feeling our introduction was over.

Looking over this powerful mustang and then over to the hands, they were as surprised as I was.

Punch handed me a blanket. I slowly approached the mustang. All hands were quiet on the rail. That mustang glanced over at me and my folly and tipped me a wink—yes, he did. I placed the blanket on his back without him flinching or raising hair.

Not a peep from the boys. I don't think they wanted to jinx me.

Punch handed me the saddle and slowly backed away. Taking a deep breath, I eased the wood onto his back. Reaching under for the cinch, "I'll just get this out of the way and we'll get this fandango on." The stallion quivered and whisked my face with his tail. I jumped back. But again, the stallion stood firm and let me lace up the cinch. I laced it real tight.

No two horses are ever the same, but this mustang was just plain smart. Holding the reins, I talked softly, slowly slipping the bosal over his nose.

I was so thrown off my game, that at best I'd be a champion or the clown. Time would tell.

With the reins in my left hand, I eased my foot into the stirrup, and grabbed a hold of his mane. The mustang shuttered and shook, unnerving me. I jerked back, "First I get on, then we play." I swung aboard quickly taking a fast set—nothing happened. "It's time to have fun." He just stood there motionless.

"Maybe he's sleeping, show 'im your boot hooks!" yelled Tank.

Hootin' and hollerin', the boys rallied with whistles and shouts, "Merry Christmas! Ya got a real merry-go-round the posies under ya."

As I sat on that stone monument, I felt foolish, but held firm knowing he had it in him . . . the mustang slowly turned his head and caught my eye with a look I'll not forget. One of the wranglers yelled, "Surprise horse. You got company aboard."

Well, that bronc flattened his ears and his nostrils flared. He swung around, hung his head, arched his back, and ignited like dynamite. He tried to fly! We left the earth like blasted rock. I fanned him with my hat and kept fanning him on every jump. He landed crooked and so hard my teeth rattled and my eyes rolled.

High and wide, jump after jump, we gained air and got to spinning in circles. Whipping up the dirt into a storm of dust, the hootin' cowboys disappeared and in the center of the blinding storm, so did my shadow. I pulled up my neckerchief and closed my eyes. I was alone in the silence of myself. Swirling around on the back of this mustang spinner took everything I had. Reaching down deep, I discovered strength I had before only imagined.

With wild, stiff-legged plunges, I thumbed him in the shoulders, and stayed back in the wood. He landed hard, time after time, popping me in the saddle. When the dust cleared, the boys cheered, surprised I was still aboard.

The mustang wheeled and bucked, scattering the hooting outfit off the corral ropes, dusting them onto the seats of their pants.

It felt like he was breaking in two. His head went one way and his hind end the other. Ernestro smiled the biggest smile and yelled, "*Vivá! Magnifico! Vivá!*"

Thinking he settled out, this sunfisher would go off again. Bucking, jumping, and twisting, he tried to flip me into the sun. He was tiring and so was I. How much more could I take? How much more could this honest pitcher deliver?—A lot!

At the top of his flight I felt it coming. With explosive energy, this high roller whirled and flipped over backwards; popping me free and clear. Falling, I watched the powerful horse tumble and bounce in a storm of dust. I rolled and landed solid right beside him straight up in my boots. "*Vivá!*" cheered El Book. "*Vivá!*"

Dazed, wild-eyed and snorting, the mustang recovered, shaking it off. Thrashing to his feet, I stepped aboard and rode him up. The outfit went off hooting and howling with ear-splitting whistles.

What this pioneer bucker hadn't reckoned on was a cowboy in love was not to be thrown off his course. I stayed steady and stuck tight in the saddle.

He whipped his head around—yes he did. He reached around, grabbed my chap with his teeth, and tried to pull me off. I hit him with my Christmas present. Boy, I hated to crease Sunny's Stetson. And, just when I felt myself slipping off, he turned good, broke into a rough trot, and smoothed out.

Yipping, hollering, and fanning their hats, the boys went wild. "*Más! Más! Más!*" shouted Ernestro.

The mustang began a parade trot with his head held high and ears straight up. Getting comfortable in the saddle, I got the feeling he was satisfied that I had qualified to enjoy the privilege of riding upon his back.

Circling the corral in a smooth trot, I smiled, looking at my shadow, realizing I had chosen well.

"*Vaya con Dios*, my friend." El Book handed me a pouch. "A wedding gift for you and your *querida* . . . my luck was good today."

I wished everyone "Merry Christmas," and said goodbye to my pards, who were all teasing, 'lover boy.'

"Merry Christmas, lover boy."

"There goes another one."

"He'll soon be roofed in, clerkin' in town at the dry goods store."

"Kiss her for me."

"Kiss your darling *querida* for all of us."

"*Feliz Navidad!*"

25

WILD RUSH

AFTER THE CIRCUS RIDE I just experienced, the trail to Santa Fe was a breeze.

Storm was quite a horse. Crouched low on his back, I imagined the riders of the Pony Express.

Storm leaped to a gallop. With the mustang's powerful strides, his nostrils flared and the musical beat of long, loping hooves pounded out a rhythm on the skin of the earth.

Blazing across the open range, I had plenty to be thankful for. My thoughts wandered over the moments I had encountered crisscrossing the far west searching for Ginny. I had experienced the awesome beauty of a land far more beautiful and bigger than any dream. And to be a part, even a small part, of something so grand humbles you in its presence and embraces your spirit.

Wild and free, I *was* alive.

In what appeared to have happened in a heartbeat,

I had experienced love and sorrow and moments of lasting memories.

The thrill of it all!

Blowing in the wind, dancing with pain, sparks and fuses, the laughter of Indians, and the stories of the *caballeros* and the ways of *vaqueros,* for the frontier wisdom and passion of cowboys generous with their lives, riding wild horses I depended on in thrashing storms, pards I had trailed and shared chuck with for the last time.

Being there was a gift.

I was alive and thankful for the motion of the moon and stars, for the warmth and glory of sunrise, and the smell of mesquite campfires and morning coffee when the sun first blinks, and everyday for the drama light plays in the skies, on the mountains, canyons, rivers, and ranges—the gold in sunsets.

Sunny was right about cowboying. I had found my way. And when I'm over and laid under, I'll be ready to cross over—now that I've ridden in paradise.

Galloping full out, riding in harmony on a free spirit across the plains, I looked up at the red-tailed hawks riding the thermals in the clear sky high above me. Glancing at my shadow with my arms stretched out like wings, I felt the wild rush.

I was flying.

Aboard this powerful horse, standing in the stirrups, raised off the saddle, leaning into the wind I crowed, "I AM A COWBOY! *Gloria a Dios!"*

My beating heart leaped with joy . . . the love of my life was just over the horizon.

26

SHINED REAL PRETTY

"ONE TICKET to Los Angeles, California on the next available stagecoach, please." Ginny had made plans to rekindle her business with Maddy and see how her investment had fared. The clerk in the Santa Fe stagecoach office looked over the stage schedule for a time and date.

"Breathtaking scenery along the way, but a rough route depending on the weather. Passengers have complained about being tumbled around and getting the sea-sickness—you may want to bring a paper sack with you!" smiled the clerk. . . .

"That will be Wednesday, a six-horse stage. An early coach, it's scheduled to depart Santa Fe half-past four in the morning. I suggest you spend the night in town so you don't miss it. Charlie tends to leave when he's good and ready!"

"Charlie! I think I've met him."

"Will this be roundtrip or—"

"One way. A window seat, thank you."

SANTA FE WAS IN A GREEN VALLEY surrounded by blue mountains. A beautiful Spanish town of flat-roofed adobe shops and houses built around a central plaza, shaded by cottonwoods.

Riding in, I passed traders and tourists, men wearing serapes, and Indian women wearing colorful woven cloth effortlessly carrying baskets on their heads filled with fruit and grain.

I made my way to the general store, which also served as the post office. I inquired about my letter of general delivery I had posted three months ago. I was surprised the clerk recalled it so quickly, "Yes, your letter was picked up just before Christmas. Nice folks, the Harts—new to the territory."

"Was their daughter with them?"

"No, sir. Just him and the missus."

My heart sunk and my face flushed. Shaken, my pale mood must have been obvious.

"Are you alright, sir?"

"Did they mention their whereabouts?"

"They didn't. You may want to inquire at Meade's Mercantile & Supply. Mr. Hart said something about digging a water well."

Just about to leave, I asked him if there was a watchmaker or jeweler in town. The clerk pointed towards Meade's. "Van Haren's. Samuel may be able to cater to your fancy. It's on your way."

"Thank you, sir."

Van Haren's shop showcased some very fine

watches. Over in the corner, some cowboys were shuffling about, anxiously eyeing a fancy wooden clock hung on the wall. Approaching the jeweler I asked, "What's all the commotion about?"

"Oh, they're waitin' on the bird to step out."

"When will that happen?"

"On the hour, every hour."

The door to the shop opened and another cowboy scooted in and walked over to the clock. "Did I miss it?"

Turning back to the jeweler I said, "It must be quite a performance."

"Since those boys come to town, they've been in here every day just before noon to hear it tweet. Now, what can I do for you, sir?"

I told the jeweler just what I wanted and he said he could have it crafted. His eyes popped when I plopped the gold nugget down on the counter. "This ought to cover it. Make it out of this, and the rest is for you."

The jeweler beamed, "Thank y—"

"Cuckoo! Cuckoo!" The bird flapped its wings, "Cuckoo!" And opened its beak with every, "Cuckoo!" The cowboys went wild with chorus—whistling, clucking, spinning around, and laughing. "Cuckoo!" I'd never seen anything like it.

Turning back to the jeweler, he smiled and repeated, "Thank you again, sir. This is more than generous."

Loaded with information, I took the wagon road north to Taos, a road of breathtaking views and vivid color. Homesteads with barbwire fences were cropping up and beginning to crowd the open range.

I spotted a pile of stacked lumber and water well casing on a ranch with an adobe home, out-buildings, and corrals. Riding up, I recognized Virgil with his Arkansas toothpick strapped to his side.

He surprised me when he spoke first. "Walker Brady! Look at you, boy. You've grown up."

Blushing, I stepped down and said, "Howdy, Mr. Hart. Good to see you." We shook hands.

"Good to see you, Walker. That's quite a horse you have there."

"He's something alright. What'cha doin'?"

"Lookin' for water." With something on his mind Virgil got right to it. "I've been expecting you."

"You received my post?"

"Oh, before that! Where have you been? Ginny was heartbroken. She ran off—it's been three years."

"Oh, no!" I was crushed. She had chosen another.

"She ran off looking for you."

"When?"

"Right after you turned up missing on the trail. She came close to finding you once, but was led astray. Can you imagine a lonesome dove like Ginny wandering around in Dodge City?"

Taken aback, I answered, "Yes, sir, I can. That would not be good."

Nodding in agreement, Virgil watched me with a serious eye.

We stood around kicking the dirt and talked for a while, catching up. I told him I had scoured the West looking for Ginny.

Off in the distance a ranch wagon was racing, dusting up the road. I was telling Virgil of my days mining for gold and growing up cowboying.

Watching the wagon get closer, "Neighbors," said Virgil. "We never did stop at the gold fields."

"What about Wickenburg?"

"Not there either. The Vulture Mine was booming, but you had to contend with the Apaches, they controlled the land."

"No wonder I couldn't find you."

Looking out at the galloping team, the wagon was drawing closer, 'Neighbors'! It was too far for me to make out her features, but I recognized the whistle. Ginny was flapping the reins and racing like she was delivering the mail!

My heart raced. Virgil and I watched as she rolled up the drive. Ginny stopped the team and sat there in the wagon just staring at us . . . My hands got sweaty and my smile got toothy . . . Ginny was just as pretty as ever.

Without saying a word, she climbed down off the wagon. She started walking, then running and by the time she reached me, she was charging with the running power of a deer.

Smiling almost to tears, "WB!" Ginny launched herself into my arms.

I spun her around to keep us both from falling.

Hugging her tightly, our hearts beat as one. "You found me." With Ginny's arms around me, we were alone and lost in each other's embrace. We hugged . . . We kissed . . . Our hearts were on fire igniting our passion.

Virgil, all smiles for the first time, raised his finger about to speak and then paused, "I'll go tell Mrs. Hart you're here. Mary will be very happy to see you."

With tears in our eyes, Ginny and I drifted off in love and caught up right where we left off.

Standing under the ramada as the sun set, Mrs. Hart called for us, "Ginny, Walker, supper."

At supper we celebrated our reunion. I played a song on the harmonica. All smiles, Pa liked my music.

Ginny smiled with an important announcement, "Mother . . . Father . . . W and I are going to—"

Virgil sprang up so quickly, his chair fell over and he surprised me with a heartfelt hug, "Welcome to the family, son." And then, hugs all around.

Virgil was truly happy I had returned.

It was good to be *with* family.

The next morning, Virgil and I were up early walking about looking for water. "Shallow or deep?" I asked.

"What's the difference?"

"If it's shallow, we'll just chase down the horny toads. They own all the surface water."

"And for a well?"

"For a well, we'll have to dowse."

I cut a fresh branch for a dowsing stick from a mesquite tree and we dowsed for water.

We familied for the next few weeks: working, laughing, planning our wedding, digging a well, raising a windmill, and sharing good times.

Ginny chose to be married in the *San Francisco de Assisi Church, Ranchos de Taos.* The priest, in jest, took pride in telling us, "The Franciscan Fathers started construction in 1772 and finished quickly, 43 years later in 1815." The Church was the most beautiful building I'd ever been in.

The sight of Ginny in the glow of the altar candles took my breath away. She was beautiful, wearing flowers in her hair. She and her mother each wore a Spanish *rebozo*—a fine silk-striped shawl, Ginny's was white. I was beaming. Mama was all tears. Pa was all smiles.

Ginny's gold wedding ring shined real pretty. I held her hand and the priest began, "Together your love will share the blessings of life. . . ."

With our vows and in the moment of, "I do," we began forever together.

I surprised Virgil and gave him a pocket watch after the ceremony. Mama wanted a portrait of the family. As the photographer was setting up his black box camera on a tripod, I asked the priest for a candle.

Hand in hand, Ginny and I held the burning candle together with Mama and Pa at our sides. And with a flash in the pan, we had our matrimonial family portraiture recorded for posterity.

27

"MERRY CHRISTMAS, COWBOY"

AFTER THE WEDDING, Ginny and I headed back to Arizona in a trail wagon pulled by the team of army mules her parents gave us for a wedding present—Roscoe and Lily.

Wandering a new trail, we honeymooned and took our time drifting southwest. The fragrance of spring was in the air. The *chuparosa* along the washes and the brittlebush were blooming everywhere. The ends of the coachwhip branches of the ocotillo were covered with bright red flowers.

Storm trotted along. He still had his spirit. I never tied, tethered or hobbled him. He was free to roam at any time. Ginny was managing the team. I was playing her a new tune. I could tell she was impressed.

The trail looked very different coming from the other direction. Nothing seemed familiar. We stopped the wagon and Ginny tied off the team. We sat there and gazed over the horizon. . . . "Sure is a big sky."

"Yes it is. And, it's all ours." We hugged and kissed.

Sitting there in God's country, Ginny noticed something. "What's that?"

Narrowing my eyes, they roved the distant hills. "What's what?" I couldn't hang my eyes on it, "What am I looking for?"

Ginny pointed, "Over there, a glint of light—a spark on the horizon. It comes and goes. You drive and I'll keep an eye out for it."

"Git up." I flapped the reins and we left the wagon road weaving our way across the range. I didn't know where we were going, but we were on our way.

The sun was high in the sky by the time I got a glimpse of what Ginny had seen miles back. Off in the distance, below the foothills of the Seven Sisters Mountains on the horizon, was a bright shimmering light. "See it?" Ginny pointed.

"I do now. It'll be near sunset by the time we get there."

"What do you think it is?" said Ginny.

Flapping the reins, "Git! We'll find out."

As we moved along, chasing the shimmering light, I remembered Sunny's words and kept an eye out for cattle on the ridges of the high country. Watching Storm, I was pretty sure there were wild mustangs around.

Off in the distance, the mountains reflected twilight tints of violet against a gold magenta sky.

Our shadows were long and violet, and the sun was three fingers off the horizon when we arrived. The shining light had disappeared miles back.

We were approaching the spot where Ginny thought the shimmering light had first appeared. Before I could stop the wagon, Ginny called out, "This is it! Whoa!"

I reined up the mules. "This is what?"

"Where we're going to live—our homestead." Ginny jumped down from the wagon. "Over there." Now running to 'over there', she exclaimed, "This is where we'll build our home . . . where we'll raise our family."

I just sat there in the wagon smiling, watching her run about. Ginny was so excited. I pulled out my harmonica and put music to her dance.

"Right here! . . . We'll build our ranch here! . . . There's lumber, land for grazing and planting, water —resources we can develop."

Ginny swirled about excitedly in rhythm with the land, plotting and planning. She slowed to a stop and looked around . . . "I wouldn't be surprised if these mountains weren't rich in silver, copper— maybe gold."

Ginny was a vision . . . and I thought out loud, "This would be a good place to call home." Jumping off the wagon, I was pretty worked up myself. "Whoa!" The chain fruit cholla Christmas tree caught my eye and stopped me in my tracks.

As I walked over to the Christmas tree, I could hear the excitement in Ginny's voice, "And we'll hang a swing on the cottonwood tree. . . ."

Abloom with blossoms, cactus wrens had made their nest with ribbons of grass in one of the branches. A rolled-up piece of paper with a string around it was stuffed into one of the cowboy boots. Pulling it out, I unwound the string. The message took me by surprise and made me smile. I rolled up the paper and stuffed it back into the boot.

Ginny joined me and took my hand. Admiring the tree's trimmings, "Your Christmas tree, it's beautiful."

"And so are you, darlin'."

Ginny removed her bracelet and slipped it onto a branch. A glimmer from the tree caught Ginny's eye. "Oh my!" she beamed with surprise, "Where did you ever find it?" reaching out to touch and spin the button.

Sure enough, and to my amazement, hanging there from a thread, was Ginny's pearl button aglow in the sunlight.

Imagine that. . . .

I smiled . . . we kissed. Embraced in each other's arms, Ginny whispered, "Merry Christmas, cowboy."

The amber bottle and jars sparkled with the sun backlighting the shimmering branches of golden thorns.

The excitement of our future together carried on as the sun set.

The Dutch oven was on the coals.

In the warm glow of the campfire, our hearts celebrated. Our Christmas tree glowed pretty with candles in the night. Forever in love, we watched the crackling flames of the fire as sparks drifted up into the desert sky to mingle with the twinkling stars.

The Moon hung bright in the western sky.

○

★   ★   ★

ABOUT THE AUTHOR

TOM VAN DYKE lives with his wife on their ranch in Cave Creek, Arizona. Tom is a nationally recognized film producer/director and award-winning screenwriter. One of his motion pictures was considered for nomination of an Academy Award®.

Tom created and wrote the American Bicentennial television public service announcements, *Stand Up and Be Counted*, featuring John Denver, the most widely viewed national and international PSAs in the history of television.

His creative expression of writing and film production is shared with his creation of fine art. Tom's sculptures, paintings and photography have been exhibited or are in the permanent collections of the NY Museum of Modern Art, the Carnegie Art Institute, the Buffalo Bill Historical Center, the Detroit Institute of Arts, the Henry Ford Museum, the Cranbrook Academy of Art, and the Butler Institute of American Art.

A Cowboy Christmas An American Tale is also available online as an audiobook, 3 hrs and 35 mins and eBook from: AUDIBLE.com, AMAZON.com, iTUNES.com